# PROSPECT

## TAYLOR HONDOS

*Taylor Hondos*

Cover Design by Ashley Ruggirello

This is a work of fiction. Names, characters, places, brands, media, and incidents are either the product of the author's imagination or are used fictitiously. Any resemblance to similarly named places or to persons living or deceased is unintentional.

Print ISBN : 978-1-927940-56-3

EPUB ISBN : 978-1-927940-57-0

*To my grandma, until we meet again.*

*Prospect*

# PART ONE

## *Prologue: Dr. Alona*

SHARDS OF GLASS covered the floor. Blood mixed with the glass, and made the sight before me look like a crime scene. One that no one recovered from. Not an inch of wood was visible on the floor. Spilt blood, antidotes, medicines and a series of different glasses covered the floor, until there was a mask of red and silver. The antidotes sent fumes into the air that made it so that I could no longer breathe without coughing after each gulp of air.

Unthinkingly, I slammed my palm into the crushed glass on my desk. It was from the latest failed attempt at an antidote. I sighed in angst. I slowly and dreadfully pulled out the jagged pieces that were smashed into my flesh.

The television hung above me on the wall. Spider cracks filled the features of the newswoman as she appeared on the screen for the latest information in town. The cracks fueled my anger from my latest rampage of destroying my lab. I was surprised that it still stood. There was nothing in the room that should have worked, but somehow it did.

There was so much depending on me, and yet so little time to fix anything at all. The news report caught my attention as it showed the news report of the first case of Dermadecatis. Isaac. He was taken into the wrong hands and I wasn't there to stop it.

Earlier that week, I had received a warning of what would come next. I knew the warning was from someone who worked for Dr. Ravana. As soon as Isaac died, the disease spread like fire. It consumed everyone around me. The letter informed me of something very important. The sickness wasn't the only issue any longer. Those with the disease would become something unthinkable. Robots. Unable to control themselves any longer. The letter didn't tell me how this would happen, but I didn't want to find out either. I had to protect my loved ones but I couldn't even fathom to begin to figure out how.

I bowed my head in my hands and pressed stiffly against my ears. I tried to drown out the sound of her voice, but it was as if the volume escalated to drive me mad. I didn't know what there was left to do. I shivered as I realized my newest failure. I let Jared down; I let my family down and ultimately, I let the world down. The destruction to come might as well have been by my own hands.

Lily, my wife, was going to die. She would be given the disease and I knew she would be the first. I knew this because the note clearly told me who would be next. If only I understood how to stop the disease, then I could save Lily and everyone in the world. I could take Lily away tonight, but I knew it would be a failed attempt. I didn't know how it would spread or how it was even contracted. There was nothing I could do at all anymore.

I slammed my knuckle down in anger hitting the glass once again. Blood poured from my hand. I watched as it streaked down beside the lines of dried blood. I glanced down to find that my white coat was bathed in red. Some blood was from tonight and some was from other nights. Cursing myself, I lifted my palm up to see the damage. I didn't care anymore so I left the jagged edges in my skin.

Out of the corner of my eye, I saw what haunted me daily. My lab was a mockery of me now. My most prized possession was destroyed and left in disarray since the outbreak. I shook my head in shame.

I picked up the shattered picture from my desk of Robert and myself. The man I once trusted stared up at me. I was unbelieving for a moment that this man was the one who betrayed me.

I let him in on my plans to save the world from all types of disease and this is how he repaid me. He grinned up in the picture and I clutched the picture, and felt the glass prick my fingers. I didn't seem to feel the pain at all anymore. I felt numb looking at the picture.

My arm was slouched around his shoulders like we were the best of buds. The truth was, we were the best of buds. We met in college and were inseparable for years.

I could not see that he was such a terrible man until now. I should have seen the signs when he continued to tell me that life was a feeble thing that could be taken at any time. He always told me that we had to take control of life and death. He used to repeat this over and over in this very room; it seemed to echo off the walls in that moment. If it weren't for Lily, I might have gone down the path he wanted me to go down.

I walked over to the second to last vial in the room that wasn't shattered. I had so much hope for this antidote. It was silver liquid as all the others had been. There was one big issue with it. It burned the skin off of anything it came in contact with.

I grabbed in from its holder and slammed it on the ground. I screamed loudly into the air as it burned against my thumb. The house was empty because Lily took Lena to the store to buy her books. Lena was always full of life, always reading, and I was going to kill her because I couldn't save her. There wasn't anything to do. She would catch this disease and she would die. Just like Lily.

I gasped as I saw my thumb once more. There wasn't skin left and my thumb bone was visible. I bleached as I backed up slowly to my cabinet full of first aid especially since I had become so reckless in here. I reached into the cabinet above me and covered it with a white cloth. It immediately turned bright red and I winced. I would have to clean this wound later but right now I didn't have time.

The truth was there was no use of trying to heal any of my wounds because I would be dead soon. I wouldn't die of Dermadecatis. That would be too easy. He would find a way to frame me into being the killer of the human race. I knew him better than he would like me to.

I began pacing back and forth. Nothing seemed to work. No antidote was strong enough. Not a single drop of one of my antidotes cured a rat, which was once the easiest to cure of my disease. Who could I trust other than Jared? He was just a child.

I wouldn't lie to myself though. I was suspicious of him at first because he was Dr. Ravana's son after all. I knew that he was true to me after a while though. He was sharper than a whip, and he was handier than his father ever was. Jared had a talent. If you told him what to build, he would do it in an instant. If you told him anything, he did it because his mind was particularly gifted in that way. I had come to love Jared as I loved his father. He was witty, and he was loyal. Above all, he was kind. He had hardened over the years that I knew came to him from his mother's death, but Jared was trustworthy. I felt it in my heart and I always chose to go with my heart now.

The main question that filled my mind daily was who could I count on to protect Lena? The whole world was going under and there wouldn't be anyone left with the knowledge of the disease. I would be dead sooner than I could decide how to cure the disease and cure the robotic mind control when that time came. Dr. Ravana would come after me. He had begun to watch the house. He wanted me dead. Who was there left that he couldn't touch? Who would I want to protect?

Lena. A voice whispered to me.

I popped my head back up. The only person Dr. Ravana couldn't harm. It would be too obvious. Her blood was too precious. She was used when we made the disease. Her blood was in the potion when we made this disease.

The disease was made to help people, to make the world a better place. I even once wanted to name it Lenima because she was the reason it was created. I created this so she would never die of a deadly disease. I created this so that all people could die from a deep slumber instead. Dr. Ravana destroyed this world and he destroyed the purity of my disease. This disease could have been revolutionary and he destroyed it.

If I could stop the disease, there wouldn't be any mind control to worry about. But what if I couldn't stop the disease? I had to try to make a remedy for both.

I stopped myself. I had to let him think he won. I had to give him hope and then take it from him as he did with my disease. If I couldn't cure the disease in time then the only thing left to stop was the mind control. I would. I would protect her from it.

I knew what I had to do. I picked up the last vile in my lab; the vile was bigger than the others that I had shattered in my fury. It was the only vile not touched by my destruction. It was like it was waiting on me to make up my mind; see the right decision, the choice that would change life forever. It would change Lena forever. The last hope, the last chance for the antidote.

I knew Lena would be punished for my own faults. I knew she wouldn't be able to understand the severity of the situation before it was too late. I hoped she wouldn't die but then I had a masterful plan come into my thoughts. I grinned widely as I began mixing and creating the last hope. I knew this would turn to dust if I wasn't careful.

I would be with Lena always and I would be with Lena when the world became too much to handle.

Who was the only hope left in the world?

Lena.

# Lena
## Chapter One: Who Am I Exactly?

THE RUBY LIGHT *was derisive to me as it moved forward. It was an unattainable chase. For hours, I continued to reach out to the light just to have it soar away from me and vanish into the distance. Although I couldn't touch it, it was always within eyesight. It floated through the air above my head. Beyond me the rosy light would reflect off the glass and blind me. After a while, I realized that this glass was a mirror, but I didn't have time to keep staring into it. I had to catch my light and I didn't know why I continued to chase it but it held an answer. I knew it did.*

*The chase seemed everlasting and wearing, but something kept me continuing on. It had to be the message it contained. I knew when the light would fade, that it would hold a secret. My breath did not falter and I wondered where this new sense of power came from. The breaths I took filled my lungs with such rich air that it felt as if I would never have to take a new breath again.*

*The light felt out of reach for so long that I gasped as I realized I was finally nearing the light, and this time it wasn't budging. I extended forward on the tops of my toes to touch it. Just as I was going to touch it, I felt something rough bump me. I looked down to see that a wall appeared. I groaned in frustration.*

*To my surprise, the light didn't move still. I smiled and licked my lips as I elongated my body over the wall. Just one touch and something would become clear to me.*

*I squealed lightly as I realized I was almost there. It slowly neared me, and I felt hope that I could finally touch the light. I leaned in some more and bit my lip as it was nearly in my hand but I felt my balance wavering too late. I collapsed face first over the wall and twisted in all directions. I smacked my face on the ground but somehow felt no real pain from it. I blustered in exasperation as I looked up to see the light had moved away and the wall I just toppled over, was gone as well. I searched my tired eyes around the room until I saw it. This time it was flashing as if it wanted to be found.*

*I followed toward it carefully. It began to move but I noticed this time it travelled slower than normal. I didn't know where it wanted me to go but I knew it was a part of me. It was a part of my life or plan. Even if it wasn't, there must have been a reason it didn't want to be caught.*

*The hunt continued as fatigue overcame me and slowed my movements. The easiness I felt earlier had completely vanished. The light stopped ahead of me, teasing me. I almost gave up but it still felt so right to catch this sucker. I moved eagerly towards it. "Got you now." I whispered through gritted teeth. I moved close to it. As I approached it, I realized it was no longer moving.*

*I stretched my hand forward, expecting the light to move away like always or for some crazy force to knock me over, but nothing came. I sighed in satisfaction as it floated into my hand. The light illuminated my hands and beamed into my eyes.*

*The beauty of it on my hand was like no other. The blushing florescent light irradiated the features of my hands. My aqua, freshly painted nails were shining in the light. I smiled brightly as I turned my hand over and over. The exquisiteness was sickening in the pit of my stomach. It felt unnatural to see such beauty in one's lifetime. No one's hand was this perfect.*

*I smiled and gazed at it. Light beamed into my eyes and I shielded myself. I looked up to find myself in front of a mirror. The same mirror I had left in my haste to chase the light.*

*The mirror revealed a gorgeous woman. Her hair was kinky with golden brown curls and pulled back with a clip to reveal her face. She was gaping into the mirror at me. The emerald color of her gown made her hazel eyed stare look forbidding.*

*I beamed at the beautiful woman and was shocked to see her grinning right back. How could it be? I was staring at myself. I was never beautiful, and I was never as elegant as she was.*

*My smile quickly evaporated as I caught sight of the light once more. The light was still illuminating my hand but I felt a sickness fall over me. This time I saw what was underneath the light. The mirror showed me the truth and what the light wanted to reveal to me.*

*The chase of the red light was to show me who I was. Under my skin was something concealed, something peculiar. My hand wasn't a human hand. It was instead a robotic arm. I continued to watch the glowing light in the mirror as I felt my mouth gaping open.*

*I was shaking and I knew this wasn't who I was. I was not an abomination like this. I looked back up to the woman who was somehow me, and watched as she shook her hand at me. She screamed loudly in my head, "Get out. I can't save you."*

*A stinging sensation ran up my spine. It shook my body severely and ran up through my hand and slammed down into my arms. I screamed loudly as the feeling of pure agony intensified. I looked down to catch a glimpse as the flesh from my hand quickly disintegrated. Inch by inch, the skin was fading and revealing silver that didn't belong to me. The sight of the metal within my skin made my stomach churn but I was too much in shock to know what was real.*

*I began to sweat as I felt heat around me. I watched in the mirror as the red light began to surround my entire body. Heat smothered me after a while and I couldn't breath. Intense pain ran all over my body. I fell to the ground as the fire began to scorch my scalp. I touched my hand to try and pat it down.*

*I watched as my hair singed clean off my scalp. I threw my head into my hands and tried to weep but no tears came. The sensation to cry made my eyes burn but no relief came as tears simply wouldn't come.*

*I took a deep breath as I realized that I no longer hurt. I no longer felt anything. I knew this was my nerve ending dying or it was the pure adrenaline warring off the pain. I dared to look at myself.*

*I took in a deep breath as I saw what I was now. I was no longer clothed. I was completely naked. My skin was replaced with metal. My eyes bulged out of the metallic circles. The fire burned around my body but it no longer hurt me. I was invincible. I was hideous. I was a monster. I was who I was meant to be.*

My body twitched as I heard loud voices in my head. "This is who you were meant to be," it shouted at me. I jolted forward and almost screamed as I watched as a red glowing light reached around me until it was beside me. My dream was real. I squeezed my eyes shut and willed the light to go away. When I dared to peek, the glow was gone.

My heart continued to pound beneath my skin. I felt the ringing within my ears and felt the batter of each beat. I cringed at my dream but I knew it was just that, a dream. I counted each pulse of my heart to remember that I was human. I had a heartbeat. I was alive and not a monster. I put my hand to my heart and paused. Beneath my hand, I felt a faint beat, even though my ears were ringing. As the beating slowed in my heart, I tried to count my heartbeats. There were only three in a minute. I felt crazy and decided that it was in my head.

Willing the crazy thoughts out of my head, I eyed the room I was in, with ivory linens all around. Everything was white, except the walls. I gripped my blanket to my chest. Everything in the room was a simple color and it strangely reminded me of a hospital except for the blood red wall in front of me. I didn't know why my heart fluttered as I imagined a hospital room. The memory flashed so quickly; I didn't get a grasp on it. My eyes flickered to a beautiful face. He had brown eyes and blond wavy hair. My hearing ability seemed to leave my body.

My dream of the chase wasn't the only thing I remembered. I had another dream. In this dream, I had been kissing a mysterious boy. What took me by surprise was the fact that his eyes were wide open as we kissed. He never blinked as he stared at me with those majestic eyes. I closed my eyes to stop seeing his stare. In that moment, I felt happiness elope around me as I realized that this was someone I loved dearly.

I reached out for him. Nothing. I looked frantically around the room for the face but I was alone. I forgot where I was because I needed to be beside him. Whoever he was. I smiled to myself.

I glanced around the room to remember where I was. The wall in front of me was ruby red. I was quickly reminded that the light I saw in my dream might have just been a mimic of this room. Then it hit me. Where was I? Nothing seemed to make sense in this moment. Why was I here and not at home? I froze in place as I tried to rack my brain of a familiar room or face. There was none. What was my home? And a better question, where was home? The only face I could seem to comprehend was the boy from my dream. I felt my breath catch as I realized that I had no answers. I could only sense that this mysterious boy was important to me.

I took in deep breaths. I spoke quietly to myself. "Okay. What is your name?" The simplest question to ask yourself and I was falling short. This is the first thing we ask someone we have just met. I didn't even have the answer to that. The first thing we notice about someone we just met is their gender and then we learn their name. I had the gender down but what was my name?

I moved my hands stiffly to my hair. My hair didn't feel ratty, even though I just had a restless sleep. I smiled as I felt the softness through my fingertips, but it froze on my lips. There was a soft cracking within my hands that didn't seem natural. I lifted my palm up to my face. I examined it ever so slightly and closely. I saw nothing but a hand, smooth and white as ever. There was nothing out of the ordinary. My dream was really getting to me. I put my palm to my forehead and quickly removed it when I felt an icy coldness erupting from my hand. I shivered in confusion but resided to putting it to my side. Out of sight and out of mind.

I lifted my eyes to assess the room more. An old, bright red jukebox stood before me. Its spotless tinted glass was brightening up the room. I jumped up to play a song, smiling eagerly. I lifted my leg from the bed, only to feel a snag and tightness around my ankle. I peered down and groaned in frustration when I realized I was rooted to the spot. A rope was fastened to my foot, to hold me in place. As if I were a prisoner. Panic grew over me as I struggled to remove my ankle from the bedpost.

I tugged and pulled and felt miserably hopeless until a new emotion came over me. I felt crazed. It was powerful and hot but a fury raged on inside me. I didn't understand this anger but it took over my insides. The rage inside me felt as if there was a large bowl of hot cement being poured over my skull. Hot and fierce, I wanted answers and I wanted them now. What was keeping me trapped in this bed? I didn't know but the fire within me was soaring down through my bones, tapping each of my bones until I jumped again with wrath. When I leaped up, the sheets beneath me dissolved and left a black scorch mark in its wake. I gasped as I threw myself to the ground from shock. I touched my leg to see where the fire came from. Was I burning and didn't even know it?

My leg was perfectly fine and intact. I shook with fear as I stared up at the music player. Confused and scared, I felt like weeping, but no tears fell this time. I was a mess inside and I knew it. I stood lightly and shook my nightgown for any shocks of smoke or scorch. I stared intently at the player.

I screeched in surprise as the music player engulfed in flames. I shouted for help but my concentration was completely on the music player before me. I tried to peer away but my eyes were locked with the player. It was as if my eyes would not break from its view. I shouted louder and finally tore my eyes from it. The corner of my eye caught sight of the flames diminishing. I had just caused a fire, I think. I shivered with fear.

I felt the world spinning around me as I walked back to my bed. I sat down afraid and alone. I gulped at the sight of the rope tied around my bed. I lifted it up to my face and gasped at what I saw. There was scorch marks along the loops. Traces of blood lined the strands.

I yanked as lightly as I could on the rope to free the rope from the bedpost it was wrapped around. The light jerk ripped the banister from my bed and I fell with a plop to the floor. I stood up slowly, registering what I had just done, but my body didn't seem like it was my own. I wobbled forward to the mirror.

As soon as I looked into the mirror, I was brought back in time to rotting around my eyes. I shook my head feverishly at the memory or maybe a foreign dream. What was happening to me? Who was I? I was just afraid.

I looked back at an alien face. She was too beautiful to be me. She had deep green eyes and flowing hazelnut brown hair, which were curled in perfect ringlets that seemed impossible since I hadn't fixed my hair since I woke up. I caught sight in the mirror of my arm. I ran my fingers over the arm and felt a slight bump. I stared down to it and frowned. There was something so familiar about it. There was something about it that made me squirm. The world before me was a mess. Wasn't it? I remembered travesties on earth before I was locked away.

There was something and I couldn't put my finger on it; something the world was fighting right outside my walls. The disease. I huffed. This was it; the world was fighting a disease. I had to help them. I felt my head feeling woozy.

I decided I would start my day. Whatever that even meant for me. I walked around the foreign room and couldn't find a trace of clothing. I felt my mouth going dry and decided to do something about my hair. I wanted it away from my face. I faced the mirror once more. I luckily had a ponytail holder.

As I attempted to put my hair up, the room seemed to spin. I felt myself losing grip. I clung to the sides of the dresser and I looked up at the mirror. Was I having a panic attack of some type? I caught sight of my eyes before I felt myself giving out. My eyes were burning a shade of emerald green and I was gone.

***

Wind whipped through my hair as I caught sight of the ground. The ground? It didn't look anything like the ground. There were pools of red all around. Maybe I was up too high and I didn't know why I was up this high either. I willed myself to see the red closer and before I knew it, I was sinking down to touch the ground. I must be dreaming because I appeared to be flying. And since this was a dream, I could do anything I wanted to do. I smiled as I glided by some odd force and reached the ground ever so lightly.

I dropped my hand down but pulled my hand quickly away as I felt the warmth of the red liquid and the smell of something toxic. Blood. It was blood. I shook my hand frenziedly and wished I had a napkin to get rid of the disgusting bile I got on my hands. I wanted to stop but something kept me going. I continued to soar, pulling myself upward, away from the blood. I searched for anything that reminded me of normalcy or the normalcy that my head allowed me to remember.

Green. I was searching for green; green trees or even green grass. To my dismay, I saw none. My mind must have been playing some cruel trick; there was nothing normal to see. Green probably wasn't even the correct color to search for. I scolded my mind internally for making me feel like I could remember something at all. All around me was darkness. Crimson, murky, obscure and auburn colors filled my features. The treetops were wilted and brown, disguising any green among their trimmings. The grass was deep black as if the sun scorched it. The sun was not out but the moon was in the sky. I pictured a beautiful scene, one with a white as snow moon, but this moon was different. The moon was cerise as if it had picked up the death and blood in the world and rolled it up to the sky to shine brightly at night.

I took a deep breath in through my nose while trying to regain some composure. The air was too sweet for me. I cringed slightly at the fact that it didn't fill me with relief, but it instead seemed to put a restraint on my lungs. There was a pressure there and I exhaled quickly. Something else was off, there was something called fresh air. It came to my mind quickly but I realized in this moment, that this air was not fresh. It was polluted with blood and casualty. The smell was bitter, it burned my nose and I held my breath with ease as to not smell it anymore. My mind wouldn't let me forget though.

The smell of burning leaves used to be my favorite scent, my darkened memory told me, but this burnt smell was nothing like this. The smell of burning of flesh and blood was something we must be born with. What I mean by this is that I think I was born with the innate sense to know what blood was, the taste, texture and, most of all, the smell. I didn't have to know that there was death and carnage all below me. Many people had died here.

I lowered myself so the trees touched my fingertips. I caught vision of a lake and rocketed over to it. I gazed into the running water. Ripples were cast through it and I smiled as I felt the breeze it presented. Now this was something that fresh air was supposed to be. It masked the scent of the air and I could almost forget what was wrong with the world. I wanted to rest and play in the water but then I saw myself. I realized that I was flying, without any help at all. I was flying by my own accord. My dream was treating me right because I was a goddess roaming through the air. I moved closer to touch the lake but as I drew near, I felt heat radiating from it. This was not normal. I grasped my hand tightly and willed myself to stop but I could not. I held my hand out in front of me to get a better look.

Red welts appeared over the surface of my pale hand. I couldn't touch water. I looked longingly at it. I stared at my reflection once more and discovered that the only thing on my back were clothes that I didn't remember slipping on.

That's when my body began to glow. The light shined and illuminated my face. It reminded me of my dream earlier. This time the light wasn't red but green. I thought maybe someone was behind me, shinning a light on me and

I looked behind me quickly to see who the trespasser was but I was alone.

My eyes glazed over as I heard voices speaking to me. *We need you now.* The voice said to me softly. I was oddly unafraid. An image of a boy passed over my eyes. His face was familiar and it brought bile to my throat as I saw him, but that feeling quickly diminished. Voices spoke softly to me, and I listened as best as I could. They were nothing but a whisper.

I felt myself being steered in a different direction but I couldn't see. My eyes were no longer working. I thrashed in the air, and pulled at my face, but it was no use. There was only darkness and it kept me from seeing my direction. I couldn't tell where I was going but the voices kept telling me it was okay. I was meeting Joseph for the next plan and that was all I knew.

Joseph was someone I trusted. I had immense respect for him. Though it didn't feel genuine. My first feeling when I thought of him had been hatred. My mind quickly dismissed this negative thought. I glided back into the air and I finally regained sight to see my destination below the trees.

I reached a house that had boards lining its windows. The house was jet black and had a gate that lined its entire perimeter. I felt scared as I saw "Freaks" written along the house but I kept my pace up towards the abandoned house and landed swiftly behind the gate. I knew exactly what to do from some unspoken bond between the voices and me.

I entered the house without turning the knob. The door quickly opened for me, and I walked towards a room where many people stood. The only light in the room was a candle burning in the corner. In the center was an older man in a white uniform; a doctor's uniform. My mind flashed to a younger face, one with no wrinkles and softer eyes although his jaw was severe and square, that looked just like his. In that moment, I felt myself smiling. I didn't know why I felt so attached to that face that I flashed to.

As I entered the room, the boy named Joseph raised his arm. All were silenced, and I tried to open my mouth to take a breath but realized my mouth was suddenly inoperable to open. I moved my hand to my mouth. Nothing was there and then my hands were pulled to the side. No one touched me though. It was as if there was some control over my body. I panicked and looked around with alarmed eyes. There were few gazes that I caught that were the same, but many were serene as ever.

The doctor spoke up and I immediately felt relieved, it was as if he reached inside me and switched my attention to only him, calming my fears in the process. He was the only thing that mattered to me in this moment. "We all know why we're here. Well most of us." He shot me a quick guarded glance, I wanted to reciprocate, but I was locked in place. My eyes were glued to him and I felt it impossible to even manage a blink. "I have selected the best of the best to come and capture some of my friends. Some of my "friends," what I mean by that is that they are my sworn enemies." Pictures flashed before my mind.

I did not know where they came from but they appeared for half a second. In that second, I had already registered exactly what they looked like from their height to their shoe size. A lump of a boy with glasses and dark hair appeared from behind my eyes as well as a picturesque girl with strawberry blonde hair. My heart ached for them but I didn't know why. I didn't know them and they didn't know me. "These are our top enemies, along with someone else. But we will save that one for last." He shot a glance over to Joseph and beamed. "Only the most worthy may capture our villain. The worthy will be prized exceedingly and will then be put in charge of things the way Joseph has earned his spot."

Shouts erupted all around me and I felt the ability of my mouth slowly coming back. I opened and closed my jaw in angst, as I hated to feel so out of control. "I want him," what appeared to be hundreds of people, shouted beside me. I watched as men brawled against one another about who was the strongest and the bravest to receive such an honor. Soon punches were being thrown because they wanted this unmasked enemy. I couldn't help but wonder what these people did to deserve this immense hatred. Everyone around me was violently angry, but I didn't feel this way towards him or her. I was overcome by the feeling that I didn't quite fit in here.

"Silence." He said it as a whisper but it rang in my ear as if he were right beside me. Again, my eyes went fuzzy and I viewed our two enemies again.

"Our newest members may be confused so I shall explain." The doctor spoke again in a whisper. He felt so close by that I shivered slightly and reached up to grab my arms and give myself a tight hug, but the blind force kept my arms to my side. "My name is Doctor Ravana. You recently were near the brink of death but I presume you have forgotten, for I have made you better. Just look around you. Well that is, when you can." He added, which showed me he was in control of my mobile movements somehow. "We are the best of the shit outside of these walls. We are the mightiest and we will be the rulers of the world. I mean it when I say we are the cure." He screamed as he smiled in triumph but I was still lost in this situation. What were we exactly? As if he heard my thoughts, he answered. "Some of you don't understand but I have been sent here to this earth to you to protect you, to save you and in turn, you will be the protectors of the world." He hesitated for a minute and I wondered if he were thinking too hard because his face looked strained.

"You will be the main protector of me. As the Greek Gods used the humans as toys, I will use you as protectors and in turn, I give you shelter, I give you love, I give you riches, I give you anything you desire and that is justly the truth. You will rid the world of the bad and the evil and I just guide you to the evil, to destroy the evil that is. For example, this fellow here," he flashed to the chubby boy," is trying to destroy you and all you hold dear. He wants to make sure he destroys every single one of you and why?" He paused for dramatic effect. "Because you have all the weapons. I have given all of you the weapons to destroy, to kill but ultimately to protect those weak and fragile." He stopped talking as he peered down at me. I trembled but stared back with a fierceness I didn't know I had.

"It is your job to find those sick and dying, and bring them to me. Or to the hospital but by bringing them to me, we are getting more bands of followers. We will guide them to protection and to be the protectors of the world like so many of you are right now. I want this man." The chunky boy appeared again. "I want him brought to me directly. I will reward the first to do it. The girl can wait, but this boy is of vital importance as I once mentioned before. Whoever brings this boy to me, will be able to avenge me when I make you search for the final target. My final target contains the highest reward. In the meantime, seek out the weak, the poor, the hungry, and the sick and bring them to me to provide them with help. I will give them their powers and then we gain our followers. Soon the world will be rid of sickness and evil."

I felt my gaze give way again and I looked around in shock. Everyone was shouting and yelling. I was no protector, I was just- Wait, who was I? I still had no idea. I looked down at my feet. High heels, a bright red were there and I wore a flowing black shirt with blue jeans. I didn't know who I was. I threw my hand up to my forehead and felt the strange coldness again. What was going on? This was a dream that I would wake from. I just had to wake myself up.

I wasn't forced to gaze up again but I listened intently, my palm still against me. "We must find these three people and destroy them. Their leader, whom is nameless right now, and themselves, created the disease that almost destroyed you. We have to protect others from it and if we can't, they must become us. They must be protectors too. I have appointed you each someone sick to rescue and remember if you see either one of the mongrels, then bring them to me as well." Screams broke out again in agreement. "Shall we?" he screeched to them. I stared up to him once more. I was mesmerized by the way the room was affected by his simple words. I realized, that I did not have an image of a sick patient to obtain, but maybe I would receive it later.

Fists were in the air and I shook my head deeply, but before I knew it, a young man was beside me, nudging me in the side before I finally raised my arm. I smiled to the boy but his eyes were glazed over and glowing. I looked on in shock, he didn't know who he was. He didn't know anything. I searched the room, but all eyes were glowing and glazed over. I realized, my eyes must be emerald as well, I didn't feel myself losing grip as I had when they turned emerald in my room.

"Miss." Someone whispered in my ear. I hopped a little in place when I felt someone near me. I looked over to see who it was. It was Joseph. I should have felt relief but I felt something different.

"Yes?" I squeaked back but broadened my shoulders and repeated myself to sound braver.

"Dr. Ravana would like to see you in his office." I shook my head feverishly as to say, "okay" and followed swiftly behind the dark haired boy that I didn't know well. My mind darkened as I remembered my bad fear of Joseph. It was like he was a monster that stole my life from me.

I stopped to watch my crew once more. Their eyes still emerald, and I decided that mine were not because I had full control over myself. The ceiling opened up, and I watched as each of their heads gazed up. I took one last look at the crowd before they all shot in the air to search for their targets. The sad thing was that they had no control over what they were doing.

# Chapter Two: Introductions

I STROLLED DOWN a tight hallway. Joseph and I had to walk in a line with me tailing behind to fit through the hall. There were not any lights and the only thing that I saw was the back of his yellow shirt. Joseph's pace was slightly faster in front of me and it reminded me that I couldn't stay in a daze; I had to keep up. I knew we reached our destination when he stopped swiftly. I almost ran smack into him but stopped myself before it happened. I shivered as to what would be behind it. Light appeared before me as he opened the door slowly. I shielded my eyes from the light bursting from the door. I squinted as my eyes adjusted to the miserable light.

He started smiling widely at me as if I was a child, and he gestured toward the double doors. I paced slowly through them. As I walked through them he stepped backward. I gazed at him curiously. "You must go in alone." His voice was barely a whisper. He passed me while brushing my shoulder slightly. At the exact moment our shoulders touched, I had a blurred vision appear before my eyes. A slightly leaner Joseph was standing before me on the roof of a car. He appeared angry and he roared out. I shook my head because I couldn't place if that image was real or not. He shut the door and I was in a dim light.

In front of me was another door. I gaped at it curiously. I sucked in my breath. I was alone and I had to be getting on with things because someone was waiting for me behind these doors. I thumped loudly on the double doors. I waited for a long while until I realized that no one was coming so I hammered more aggressively. As my knocking dissipated, I saw the imprint of my fist engraved into the door. I jerked back in embarrassment. I had strength running through my veins that I knew was abnormal. The powers the Doctor had given me were unnatural.

The door opened finally, and my breath caught as a stunning man walked towards me. He had a turquoise button up shirt on, and I could see that the sleeves tightened around his arm muscles. I coughed in embarrassment as I caught myself staring a second too long. This was the boy. The boy I continued to have visions about and dream of for three nights straight. Light shinned on his eyes and my heart faltered. This wasn't him.

The boy I dreamed of had eyes that made my knees weak. The boy from my dream's eyes was not black with a hint of vindictiveness as this boy's eyes were. They had bitterness to them that my dream boy could never obtain. His hair flowed exactly the same way but his height was off as well. My dream boy had height that towered over me and I didn't mind in the least bit. This boy was short. He slightly overpassed my height.

"Hello." He paused as he looked at the door in shock. I scowled a little because I was making a fool out of my self for almost beating down the door. "Eager to meet us, I presume?" he chuckled lightly. My heart picked up because he so reminded me of the dream.

"Why, I don't know why I have been sent here. There was a voice talking in my ear after I had been dreaming. It woke me up. I was dreaming of someone." I said awkwardly. I stopped talking and looked down. The dashing boy walked to me and placed a hand on my shoulder. It seemed to burn within me, my face flushed but I tried to keep a steady stance to not give me away.

"My name is Aiden. I do not know your name and I think you are unsure of your name as well. Let us help you." He threw his hand behind him and towards the man in all white, which just spoke to the crowd. "This is Dr. Ravana. We want to help you discover who you are and what your purpose here will be." He smiled and it gleamed in the light. I was shocked to see how calm he was in the situation that he was a sending many off to find people. To kill them or to trap them, I was not sure.

"How do you do?" I said politely to him. I bowed to him, but it felt foreign for me. I did not know who he was but my mind told me to bow, and so I did. If I wouldn't have bowed, I was sure that some force would have made me to anyways.

"Perfect. Tell me everything you can remember before today." I shrugged because that seemed perfectly easy to do but I stopped heavy in my tracks. Yesterday? Yesterday I was- wait. Where was I?

I walked slowly into the room as Aiden signaled for me to come inside. I quickly began explaining myself. "Dr. Ravana. This seems insane but I do not remember where I was or who I am. I remember waking up to a room. A red room and I remember dreaming of this wondrous man. The thing is, sir, I can remember a dream I have had repeatedly, but I cannot remember anything other than the dream. I do not remember the days revolving around those dreams. I know that I have had the dream at least three times. This man, he seemed close to me. I know he means something. He must." I grinned deeply to myself. This boy meant something. "I have also had a dream about a red light. I think that was just a random dream. But this boy, the boy I dream of, he is all I can remember of the past."

I looked up to Dr. Ravana. The look on his face was pure insanity and rage. He caught my stare and his smooth exterior returned. "Well." He said acidly. I was confused by his anger and my muscles clenched. "I think this boy is a figment of your imagination. I mean this in the nicest way. Could you describe him?" I closed my eyes so that all my senses could reach the man I dreamed so dearly of.

"He's tall and has wavy hair. Just like Aiden." I looked toward him, and he looked away to meet Dr. Ravana's glance. I continued on. "He wears combat boots and he just seems so familiar to me. His eyes are brown. Come to think of it, they made my heart flutter." I felt heat around me when I remembered where I was. I quickly stopped telling them how in love I was with his eyes. I huffed slightly and continued. "They sparkle and his square jaw compliments his eyes because he looks angry all the time but his eyes soften him."

Dr. Ravana seemed to shake with anger and I couldn't understand why. His hands were by his side in fists and I realized that this meeting wasn't going well so far. "I think that we need to talk about this. This is not okay to dream. My followers do not dream." He shouted, "Do not" loudly causing me to jump. "There must be something seriously wrong with you, my dear." I was shocked by his tone. It was menacing and I shivered with fear. I could feel the chill bumps rising within my arms but when I looked down, I found none.

Dr. Ravana never looked away from me. His eyes bored into mine, and I found myself in a daze. I didn't move and felt rooted in that spot. He got up slowly and moved towards me. I felt like cowering away, but I didn't because an unforeseen force held me up right. Chin up, eyes staring wide, and I watched with self-aware eyes as he moved to Aiden and spoke in a hushed tone. His eyes never left mine, and I stood up straighter without hesitation as he lifted his finger in an upward motion.

My feet moved before I could comprehend anything. On unsteady legs, I walked quickly to the murky brown bookshelf beside the desk. There was nothing on the bookshelf except a globe and an encyclopedia. I spun the globe around. It was as if my body knew what to do before my mind did and before I knew it, the bookshelf shifted to the left. I didn't know why I knew this would happen, but I stepped through as Aiden followed. The force I felt before was gone and I turned to Aiden. He was smiling in a peculiar way. "What is it?" I asked in a small voice. I felt as if I were in a dream. I couldn't think straight anymore. The room was small and had a musky smell in it. I didn't want to be here, I realized in that moment.

"What am I doing here?" Panic was rising in my throat but I attempted to keep it down. I was hoping I could get something of a response for once.

"We are just running a few tests." He hesitated, but his eyes never left mine. They were so intense but something was off about them. The boy in my dream was different. He made me swoon. Aiden made me feel peculiarly sick. I didn't like his stares.

He inhaled deeply and his mood switched from apprehensive to composed. "We are finding out who you are and who your first target should be. You are having dreams, which is something you can not do." I felt frightened because I didn't remember much about life before now but I did know that dreaming was something I should do. He continued on as my head swirled with wonder. "We have a number one target and we still haven't found someone worthy to find him. We have a strong feeling it is you." His eyes twinkled and his eye twitched ever so slightly.

This was alarming to me because at that exact moment, I was reminded of someone who was lying. A needless twitch, a sign of lying, an angst in the making, was associated with twitches to me. I didn't have time to decide if he were a liar or just someone who was naturally nervous because he was coming towards me. I was spooked and tried to shift away from him but I couldn't. He grabbed my upper arm, hard. It felt as if his fingers were going through my skin. I wanted to shout but he put a hand over my mouth. My breath was ragged and I wanted to bite down on his hand. That was when he pulled his hand away and pulled me fiercely to his face. I could smell his fresh mint breath as he caressed my cheek.

Bile rose in my throat. I felt as if I were really going to get sick right there. If he tried to kiss me, I would probably deck him right there, or at least try. I felt afraid but my body could not move. He looked deeply into my eyes and I saw from the corner of my eye that he was raising something towards my face. I felt the prick on my forehead a moment too late. He moved me to the chair behind him and I felt myself losing grip. The last thing I saw was the syringe he was holding as he smiled sinisterly in my direction.

# Chapter Three: Captured

I SHOT UP awake in the gloomy, dim room alone. Different voices screamed in my head, bickering back and forth where to find the target. I placed my hands on my ears to drown out the noise. There was a voice that was calm and serene, and I focused in on his voice and it said, "You are worthy of this target."

I shivered as I searched around the room and found that I was only greeted by more darkness. My eyes couldn't seem to adjust to the dark and I felt frustrated. That was when I heard a door opening. As if by magic, my eyesight returned and light reappeared to me.

Aiden was smiling at me with a menacing grin, the exact same one he left me with. I couldn't help but feel a little bit leery of Aiden and it distressed me how daunting he was. "It turns out that you are worthy of the main target." It was as if he had been the one chanting to me in my head. I didn't budge as he drew closer to me. I began chewing on the inside of my mouth from my nerves.

I sighed slightly in frustration, but his stiff stare made me stop short. He continued on as I smacked my lips together in silence. "He is of utmost importance to this entire process. If we were to capture him, then the world would be safe once more." I felt my forehead screwing up in confusion, and he seemed to notice. "I know you're confused. It will all make sense to you eventually. The truth is, you probably won't capture him tonight, but you must try as hard as you can because he is so important to the human race. He is the difference between destruction and restoration." This was all so confusing. I felt a little out of place. Why was I needed here at all?

"I am sending you information right now." He walked swiftly over to the small desk and typed quickly into the laptop that sat across from me. "You might feel a little odd," he paused as he searched for confirmation as he used that delicate word, "when you get it but do not be afraid. You will experience heightened senses to reach this man." I raised my eyebrow as he said the word, "heightened," but he persisted on. "Yes, our target is highly lethal and you must be prepared to destroy him if he tries to hurt you and he will try to hurt you." He nodded in encouragement and I knew then that my face was showing how frightened I felt.

I couldn't be afraid. I didn't know what was going to happen to me or why I was chosen for this task but I had to be strong. I had to be brave because this appeared to be my life. I didn't know who I was but that gave me power. Power to start over and be the bravest, strongest person I could be.

For the first time, I knew that I was going to have to prevail any apprehension that I had. "I'm ready to fight." I said with confidence. Aiden looked on with captivated eyes.

He nodded slightly and pressed on with his instructions. "Your target doesn't need a name. I find it easier to not give them names in case emotions get in the way. Sometimes a name will attach you to a memory of someone else with that name. In this field, it is best to be without emotions and only run on logic or physical attributes."

I nodded and showed that I understood him. "You will be given his location and when you finally begin to approach him, you will finally see his face to recognize him. We used to show only coordinates and then some people would grab innocents." He shook his head lightly as if he were trying to forget a bad memory and spoke with care, "we definitely do not want that to happen again." For some odd reason, my mind was screaming at me that he wasn't sincere, but it quickly passed. I shook my head to try to rid myself of such nonsense. "Now, here are his coordinates." I jumped at the sound of his voice but then my brain became a fuzzy mess as numbers appeared before my eyes. Out in front of me, I saw numbers "37 N, 120 W."

"This is very important, you have to find him and locate him using those coordinates. You don't have to attack tonight. Just find him and watch him from afar. Get familiar with the town he is in. Connect with people if you can." He stopped typing and turned to face me. He even stepped away from the desk. "If you fail in this task, you will not be allowed to come back. I know we gave you the toughest person and task, but we have to weed out the weak. We just want to get this guy off the streets. So try your best, Miss. Honestly, the big man will probably take it easy on you since it is such a big task." He looked at me intently, and had a knowing, kind of smile. I couldn't help but smile back as my lips trembled, when he looked away I felt disgusted. I would be thrown out into the street if I didn't succeed?

He walked slowly to me and extended his hand out towards me. "Ready?" He asked tranquilly.

"For what?" I asked a little too cautious, as I reached for his hand as well.

As soon as my hand touched his, he grimaced and took a deep breath. "I gave you the coordinates but I was going to try and help out by giving you an extra boost of knowledge. I am going to show you the landscape of the town, just to help out." Then he pulled my hands slightly as I reached up and I found myself leaning in closely to him.

He put his mouth to my ear. I felt the heat brushing through my body and burning my ears. "I am helping you out in a bigger way than I have ever helped anyone before," he whispered so faintly, that if a pen dropped at this exact moment, I would miss it, "you are very special, and I don't want to lose you being around." He moved back and I realized in that moment that my ears were pounding in the silence. I reached down to feel my chest and felt my heart pounding beneath my hands. I wanted to smile by being able to feel my heart but I was afraid he would confuse it for flattery. I was glad when he stepped away because he might have heard my heart pound through my ears.

He spoke loudly once more, "Now, are you prepared to have the rest of my information?" I nodded and I sat back down slowly. I closed my eyes, while taking a big breath in. Before I knew it, my head was tingling in an "odd" way as he termed it before.

The town was fifty miles from where I sat at this exact moment. There was a quant town and I beheld flashes of a town square. I was startled as my mind narrowed down to a single image. There was a town square, and it showed me of its destruction. It was demolished, I didn't know from what, but the townspeople were working to make it whole once more. The small town was familiar in a way but I couldn't place it in my mind. I felt anger coursing through my body but I couldn't place the wrath. I believed that it was because these people were hosting my newfound enemy. These people were my enemies too, every last one of them. I would destroy them because I had to. It was my job.

"Now. This is where you must go. Make friends." He chuckled lightly and I tried to look up to him but just then, my eyes were blinded once more. A rough hand grabbed me up from the chair I sat and stood me upright. The hand held me tightly as if I were a rag doll, unable to stand on my own, unable to think on my own.

Aiden spoke quietly, he was close to me but I still could not see. "Now answer me this." He whispered it and I shivered. "Do you remember a dream anymore?" My dream boy flashed once more in my mind. A laugh on his lips and I felt my stomach flip.

I decided to lie because I didn't want him to be taken from my mind. "No. I don't even know what you're talking about."

He spoke once more making my head spin. "Do not disappoint the Doctor. He does not give second chances." I trembled with dread because if I were to disappoint him, I would be alone and afraid. Then a thought erupted and it rang true, the strength I held was coursing through my veins and I could take an old man like him.

"I won't disappoint." I said it before I even thought of saying it, what frightened me was that I didn't recognize my own voice. I felt heat emitting from my body, and finally could see again. I couldn't see it but I knew it was happening. I was glowing once more from my body. I knew if I were seeing myself through someone else's eyes, that I was glowing emerald green. I was ready to discover my target.

I felt myself lifting from the ground and I smirked at the power I possessed. I flew along the walls until I swooped underneath a table, which opened up the ground underneath it. I was flying through a dark tunnel. I must have been here before because I knew where I was going without fail.

I felt the breeze of cold air even though my body was full of heat and anger. I couldn't help my feelings. I felt a fury that I couldn't place the origin of, but I was going to use it against my target. After all, Aiden said not to attack tonight, but he didn't say not to kill tonight.

***

I was in the mysterious town in an instant. It seemed as if I were teleported there instead. The air was heavy with a sort of fierce belonging and immediately I felt that I didn't belong or fit in to the square of destruction. I soared through the outskirts of the town and landed in a tree. I searched for a sign of movement and found that there was none.

I steadied myself in the tree before I dropped down abruptly and caught myself as I landed straight on my feet with ease. I chuckled out loud to myself. This could be fun; the power that Dr. Ravana gave me, didn't seem so bad.

"Lena?" I heard a voice call and I kept walking absentmindedly. I continued on my way, turning to the left and a sudden weariness covered me and I felt like I was being followed. I peeked around and found that no one was there.

Just when I was in the clear, I heard the voice speak again. "Lena?" This time it was a little louder and somehow sounded more confirming than a question ever should. A girl with bright red hair approached me. She reminded me of a clown. Her hair was unnaturally red, as if she had dyed it. The smile on her was sickening, and I felt my stomach twist. She was a slender thing and I had a gut feeling that I knew her.

I stared deep into her eyes, which were a beautiful blue color. I racked my brain for some clarity, but there was none. "It's you." She stopped slowly and stared me up and down; not in the way I wanted to be stared at. She stared deeply into my eyes. "What have they done to you?" she said with a repulsed tone as she stepped back afraid. I felt my breath hitch in my throat from her revolted way of speaking to me.

"You have the wrong person. I am not a Lena of which you speak of." I said plainly and turned so that I could continue on my way. I felt a tight grip around my arm and felt myself being spun around. I didn't get angry but I felt violated. Who was this girl to speak to me or touch me in any way at all?

"You even talk different. You sound like a.." she stopped in her tracks and I thought I even saw tears welling into her eyes. "You're one of them." She started pacing and seemed to be hyperventilating. I laughed at the sight of her panic.

"Miss. Calm down. I can help you find Lena. I really am not her. I am sorry." I reached out to touch her but she shrank back.

"Oh no. Don't touch me." she began crying and I shrank into myself. I wrapped my arms around me as if that would protect me from her. I needed to get away because she clearly wasn't sane.

"Miss." I tried one more time, and she suddenly jerked her head up with a villainous smile on her. Her face froze. I tried to wave goodbye to her because it was all too creepy for me but just as I lifted my hand, a power beyond me pulled my arm down. Her stare was menacing but I felt the wave of control that I felt in Dr. Ravana's mist but this was a little different. It was less sincere and welcoming.

She laughed at me and broke her gaze. I felt the unknown spirit being lifted, and I gasped for air. It truly took my breath away to be under that control. I looked once more over at her and felt my breath take once more. The flaming red hair that she had finally seemed to suit her. Her once beautiful sea blue eyes were taken over by a fury. It seemed to turn her eyes into a red, not just any red but a red the color of pools of blood. "I never liked you anyways." She whispered it, but it pierced through my skin.

"You have the wrong girl." I said a little frightened. Her eyes didn't change back to the color they once were.

Before I knew it, she was screaming. Not just any scream, but the scream of a banshee, the true omen of death. I cringed and felt as if I were going to pass out but then she was shouting and I could make out what she was saying.

"I have another one." She yelled in a menacing way. "And this one will be fun."

Before I had time to use my new talents to just get the hell away from it all, I was being pinned down. Before I knew it, cloth was going around my head. Darkness covered me and I smelt the smell of a bitter tomato. Arms were holding me in all types of ways, but I wasn't even fighting them. Their grips were strong and uncomfortable, but to a normal person, these hands might have been hurtful.

That was when someone smacked me in the back of the head. I saw spots fill my eyes and heard the grumbles of a man saying to me "Stop resisting." Even though I wasn't in the least bit. I gritted my teeth and knew that if he wanted to see a real resistance, then he would get one.

The fury gathered behind my eyes. I felt my head radiating but unlike in my room, nothing blasted away or even began to melt. That was when I felt the blasts coming right back to me. I screamed in excruciating pain as I felt the explosions coming to me because they wouldn't burn through the sack on my head.

I felt a stronger hit to the side of my head and I screamed out in pain. Would I die right here? I knew I could fight them off. I had the strength, I knew I did. That was when someone pushed hard onto my right arm, it was a tender place, probably from my past life but it was the most unbearable pain of my life. The pain rippled all the way up to my head and I actually thought I would die in this very place, at that moment.

"Who are you?" I finally gasped out in agony.

"We are the Earth Saviors. We are the protectors. You and your kind have been around for too damn long." The fiery red haired girl yelled to me. As if a child, I felt her foot nail into my knee. I didn't even flinch from the effort. I laughed at her pathetic combat skills and her attempts to hurt me.

I opened my eyes wide and realized I could barely make out her face. It was drawing closer to me and I moved through the pain of my arm. I lurched back as fast as I could and as far as my guard would allow me without noticing and punched the girl in front of me. I watched delicately as I saw something splutter from her nose, and I knew I hit the target. That was when the guards instinctively let go of me to see if their leader was okay. I punched again and this time found it was a new nose, a more delicate crunch this time.

I heard screaming coming from in front of me. It was coming from whomever I hit. "Kaley!" she screamed loudly. "My nose is broken! Help! Oh my god! " She shouted as I watched through my sack as she slammed to the ground.

The red head, by the name of Kaley, reached down to pull on my other victim's hair. "Get up." Kaley shouted in outrage. "Get up or leave this group now, you coward."

I pulled the sack off my face while I had time and watched in horror as my fingers began to melt in a sickening way. The skin was peeling so profusely. While blood should have been pouring out of my skin, there wasn't. Although my eyes didn't burn through the sack, they most certainly heated the bag up. I closed my eyes and smiled to myself as I realized that the pain was dissipating. Not only was the pain disappearing, but also my skin was growing back in seconds.

I smiled deliciously as I saw more flames approaching me. Obviously fire, burning, melting or heat didn't bother my new body in the slightest way. There was a streak of pain that vanished quickly. Every single one of my attackers held a blowtorch.

In some sick way, I welcomed the flames; they seemed to renew something in me. I wanted to see how much my body could take without breaking down. That's when they all threw the fire death sticks at me. Smoke erupted around me and I felt heat. There was a nibble of pain but then it quickly stopped. I was being burned alive but it didn't hurt me in one bit. The fire was not painful; it was as if a bite of heat was touching me instead.

I looked around me and saw that where I stood, there was a circle of no fire. The flames would not touch me and I laughed cruelly at them. I took a deep breath, hoping the flames really were my friends as I walked through them. I prided myself to see the looks on the "Earth Saviors" faces. Kaley was in outrage.

"Lena Alona. We will meet again. You can count on it. You will die and I swear to God it will be by my hands. You're a monster now and you always were. That's why mommy and daddy died, so they could leave you. You bitch!" She spat at me.

I beamed again at her and tried hard to mimic the intimidating smile she wore not too long ago. The wrath I felt for this whole situation and the name she called me finally starting to build in me.

I felt my eyes burning and I stared intently into her eyes as I had this morning in my room. Finally flames erupted around the ground where she stood. I just wanted to scare her but when I saw she still didn't falter in her stance, I felt that it wasn't enough to just scare her. I had to punish her. I had to make sure these people didn't bother me during my task.

"You and your people need to steer clear of me. Do you understand?" I said in the crisp voice. She didn't respond, instead she stood taller and lifted her middle finger to me.

"Lena. Go to hell." That was enough for me. I reached beside me and I took the flames and held them in my hands. It tickled my skin and I laughed down at my new friend.

"Well, you really shouldn't have said that." I said and then I released the flames. They crashed into her and she fell to the ground. All her followers crowded around her and I chuckled as cruelly as I could, which wasn't hard. My heart felt evil, but I had to be the boss around here and not them. At least I gained one thing from this red headed devil. My name was Lena.

## Chapter Four: The Target

AS I FLEW above the trees, I watched as the crowd grew around Kaley. Some were facing up to me and I could see their resentment of me all over their faces even from up here. I smirked down at my burning friend. All around her, people were stripping out of their clothes so that they could begin to pat her down with their jackets or articles of clothing. Men stood practically naked in the streets to get the fire out. From here, I could see that she no longer had a lot of hair. The right side of her head had not one speck of hair left. It was all singed off. She cursed into the air as she flopped uselessly on the ground.

I gazed down at my body, which stayed untouched and unfazed by the flames. In that moment an unearthly thought came to mind, I owed this man. Dr. Ravana had given me powers that I could only dream of. I would use them for good. Well, I would use them against my enemies too. I continued to watch them and felt a little alarmed at how easy it was and how unaffected I was by the turn of events. Shouldn't I feel a little remorseful for what I had just done to these people?

I didn't have time to feel bad. I had to remember my purpose here. My exchange had me unfocused and I had to remember my goal. The remorse would have to come later if it ever did. In my mind, I could see coordinates reappearing in my thoughts. My unidentified target was close by. My eyes blurred as I saw the coordinates. They seemed a little bit different than before. Before I knew it, I was being steered in a new direction. I felt like panicking but then my eyesight returned and I realized I was flying in the opposite direction of where the girl on fire stood. This must have meant my target had already left his original spot.

I flew through the town, and all I saw were the mulled buildings once more until I approached a neighborhood. Only five houses were left standing while the rest of the houses seemed to have been obliterated. On the remaining ruins of homes, there were words. I caught sight of one. "The Earth Saviors Were Here." Kaley and her weird band of followers came to mind. They seemed to be doing more bad than good.

I continued to search around. There was debris all around. In the pit of my stomach, something seemed to harden and I lurched forward. I didn't understand but I felt anger coursing through my veins. I landed lightly on a house with a forest green roof, which I felt was an odd color. The house across from me was gigantic. There were white shutters on the blue house, with a porch on the second floor.

It was beautiful, and I couldn't help but feel a comfort when I looked at it. I felt captivated and somehow connected to this house. I stared at it longer. I decided that if I didn't have a home already, I would want this to be my home. It was everything I wanted. It gave off a feeling of home.

There was a trigger in my head, and I felt as if I was being pulled from the roof. My eyes blurred once more and I was being moved again. I was walking and not flying. I was grateful for that. Then I stopped and I could see once more. I was still in view of the blue house, but I could see a new side of the house. The blue house had a side walkway that led to a door. By this door, there was a beautiful garden. There were pink flowers peaking through. This could only mean one thing; it was springtime. I wanted to rush down to look closer but I couldn't. I looked to the yard and saw a swing set and I felt my throat constricting. For some reason, I felt emotionally attached to everything around this house.

I knew that I wanted to stare at it forever and learn everything about the people who occupied this house, but then I saw movement. I crawled to the edge of the house and hid behind the bump in the roof and the chimney.

The front door to the house creaked open and it looked as if the door were examining the outside before peering out to say "hello world." I wanted to chuckle at myself but then a shadow approached the door. A boy with combat boots, jeans and a black tee shirt stepped out. He kneeled abruptly on the ground and touched the side of the house as if he were trying to caress it.

I wanted to giggle at the sight but I was too mesmerized by him to shift or make a sound. I realized then, that he was trying to do something to the house. I listened, realizing my ears could be heightened in this sense as well. He started groaning to himself and cursing but he stopped himself short. He immediately stood as if a bee stung him right on the behind and he turned slowly. The turn was bitterly slow and I felt like he knew I was there.

I didn't budge when his face turned up towards the sky. He looked straight at the bump that I hid behind. I wanted to peek around to get a closer look, but I could see past the bump enough. He kept his gaze on the chimney and I felt my breath catching. I felt explosions go off in my head as he turned his entire body around to face the house I was on. This boy was something like a dream. Better yet, I was willing to say he was the boy from my dreams.

He quickly turned back to the house and walked with extraordinary speed to his house. I didn't want to move, but my legs were cramping. I got up and shook my legs out to get out the kinks and was ready to get a better hiding spot along a tree in the yard when I saw him. I stopped in place and felt panic in my throat.

He stood perfectly still on the roof in front of me and stared at me as if I were the only thing in the world. He looked at me as if I were the most recognizable face he'd ever seen. There was a great distance between us but I could almost feel that he was right beside me. That was the type of warmth he was giving off to me. I shuddered at the thought of me being beside him. I wanted that.

He waved to me on the roof and I was feeling bashful but threw a hand back. He must have known that I was there before and he was probably curious as to why. He didn't go about his business but instead continued to stare.

That was when signals went off in my head. Bile burned in my throat, as I looked deeper at him. I felt signals go off in my head as the strange voices returned. "Initiating target," it whispered to me.

I stood up taller and looked deeper at him. The boy from my dreams was my target? How could that be? He did not look like my enemy but then again, the people on the street did not appear to be either.

I felt strongly for this boy and it made anger build inside me. I had no idea why but I felt that I really knew him. I felt love for him but there was confliction in my mind. The voices exploded louder and I covered my ears. They screamed for me to know that this is the target. I was the only person worthy of this target. I had to act natural so he didn't suspect that I was going to come and kill him eventually. I took my palms from my ears and swapped my hair to the side to pretend that was what I was up to, to begin with.

I calmed down but the voices did not stop. They were quieter than before but they still reminded me of the enemy before me. He looked concerned when I lifted my head back up but I sat down to act as if I belonged to the house in which I stood on.

He walked closer to the edge of his roof and I felt butterflies. I willed them away because this was the target I would have to kill. It would be hard to kill something so beautiful.

"New to the neighborhood?" he smiled over at me in a knowing way and I couldn't break my strength.

"You could say that." I said as sweet as my voice would allow.

He stopped his stride short when I spoke. A strange look passed over his face and I looked on in admiration, internally slapping myself square in the face.

"You seem different." He said calmly and I was struck by this comment because this stranger seemed to think he knew me. I was about to shake my head to tell him he for sure didn't know me but then he spoke. "What's your name?" he said to me, curbing my discomfort at him believing he knew me.

"I don't talk to strangers." I said in a charming way, and I was quickly reminded of how women try to flirt. I didn't want to become that. I didn't even know how to do that, come to think of it.

"I see. Well, I don't want to bother you ma'am. I just wanted to say, you look absolutely beautiful on the roof with the sun shining on your pale skin." He bowed gracefully with a wide smile on his face, as if he were telling a joke. I couldn't help but smile back and I was struck how familiar his actions were. I felt my heart patter against my chest. I was happy to feel that patter, it seemed as if I never felt that anymore.

How was I going to kill him? I had to because it was my duty to protect the world from the number one enemy. I couldn't let Dr. Ravana know that I communicated with my target; I would for sure be thrown out of the group.

He continued to stare at me, a laugh playing on his lips. "Have a nice day." I couldn't help it. I felt blood pounding to my face.

"Thanks." I said and it was barely audible as I watched him crawl back to the window by the roof and he returned back into his house. I shuttered at the thought of killing someone; especially someone who looked like him.

The saying might be true that evil is normally disguised by beauty.

# Chapter Five: Unbreakable

I FOUND MY way back home. Well, I didn't exactly know how to get there, but my mind somehow took over as soon as I thought to myself, "how will I even get home?" and suddenly I was landing on top of the glass building. I reached the side of the glass building to find a door open. It was as if the building had one opening and it was only to my room.

Once inside the room, I realized how out of place I felt. It didn't feel like it belonged to me. My mind continued to race. Why did that boy have to be so intriguing? I couldn't help but feel attached to him.

I closed my eyes and lowered myself to sit slowly onto the black bed. I smoothed the comforter beside me and leaned back onto the bed. I looked to my side and was captivated by the exquisiteness I saw. My room overlooked the ocean and the room was completely open due to the glass all along the left side. Normally this would have bothered me, but the only thing that would see me was the ocean. I stood quickly to shut the door that had let me in and felt the breeze was somehow welcoming to me. I felt alone except the air felt like an old friend to me.

The house appeared to be floating over the ocean. I didn't care that it wasn't possible; it was how it seemed. I wanted to believe that I belonged here but so far I wasn't so sure.

I beamed at the serene feeling of the ocean but as soon as the door hit to close, noise erupted all around me. I jumped in place as I heard people talking, screaming and laughing. I had to see what was going on. I walked slowly to the white door that seemed to hang awkwardly in the room. I unbolted the door to peer out into the hallway, expecting to see some faces. There was none.

I took a deep breath and walked towards the end of the hallway. I was surprised to see that my room was the only door around. I continued walking but didn't see anyone or any rooms. I had just heard talking, and I didn't know if it was just in my head. I turned the corner and that's when I saw them. There had to be fifty doors down a long, wide hallway. Glass still surrounded me and I could still see the ocean. Where was I? Why was I secluded from everyone?

I was alone in the hallway until there was a buzzing in my ear and every single door opened synchronized. I stood frozen as a ton of people strolled out of their rooms; they all walked past me in the hallway. All of them held books in their hands. I looked for a familiar face but I saw none. I frowned; how was it that I didn't even know the people that lived with me? They all talked amongst themselves.

Many people nodded to me as I passed and I tried my best to give the best smile I could muster, but I felt too grim. What was this place? It seemed like I was in a dorm hall.

Then a laughing crowd passed me and some even said hello to me. I decided to follow them and listen. I was going to pretend that I belonged even if it killed me to know I didn't at all.

"Did you see their faces last night?" a boy with dark green hair spoke. He was very handsome but his hair was too strange for my taste.

"She was so afraid and she screamed, "No, don't hurt Gabe."" A girl with a leather jacket told them animatedly as she lifted her hands up in surrender. They all laughed loudly. They must have found their targets. I grinned a little. I found mine, and they must have talked to their targets as well. At least I wasn't breaking the rules more than anyone else had.

"Did you talk to them?" I spoke up before I could stop myself.

All pairs of eyes scanned me. Worry crossed the green haired boys face before he spoke. "No. Of course not." I felt my face fall. He must have noticed because he stepped closer with a finger waving like a mother to a child. "You are not supposed to treat them like they are worthy of speaking to. We are only allowed to talk to certain targets. Ones that we want to become one of us." He took another step forward towards me with a menacing look. "Why? Did you talk to a target? You wouldn't want anyone to know. Now would

61

you?" The others ganged up behind him, and I wanted to cower down but I refused to.

I didn't answer yet. "Well, answer us." A girl with a pink streak in her hair said as she stepped even closer to me.

I was baffled. I caught my breath and stepped to them unafraid. I was nose to nose with the odd green haired boy. "No and why would I tell you anyways?"

"I think you need to watch who you talk to. You're new around here but I am in charge for getting many people here." I smirked because he wasn't given my target anyways.

"Oh yeah?" I backed up to watch his reaction. "I was given the number one target." He gasped in shock and I smirked in the delicious truth in his eyes.

He turned to face the others and recognition triggered in their eyes. He bowed down to me and the group followed. My mouth fell open. "You are the one we were waiting for then." I felt my face screw up in shock. They were waiting for me?

"Why on earth would you be waiting for me?" I screeched out and wanted to hit myself. I was worthy and I needed to act like it.

"You can change the world. Make us all the rulers. Please tell me your name. I must know it." He told me quietly as possible. I didn't see the crowd forming behind him and his crew until now.

"Get up please." I said calmly.

"Nice to meet you "Get up Please." They all chanted behind him, and he smiled up at me while still bowing. *For the love of God.*

"Please." I said even though I wanted to laugh. I didn't understand but I recoiled down. "Can we go somewhere to talk?" I asked him quietly, I felt the crowd closing in and I needed to be away from their eager faces. He shook his head willingly while finally standing up.

He grabbed my hand as he weaved us through the crowd as each of them tried to touch me as if I were a famous person. He led me down a hallway and we reached a door. It looked just as mine did in my room, awkward as can be sitting upon the glass wall. I felt my breath take but then I saw the sky. The sky was bluer than any blue I had ever seen. Or had seen in a while.

I felt as if I was floating, but then we were approaching a red bridge. I walked ahead of him and realized that we were walking on a bridge over the ocean. I was absorbed in the beauty.

I reached my arms over the side before I felt a firm grasp on my arm. "Careful." He let go quickly and instead he held his arm to block me. "Don't let the water touch you." I looked questionably down to the ocean.

"But the ocean is harmless." I said. I remembered faintly that I used to swim in this.

"Maybe once before. But now it burns like a bitch if it touches you." He hesitated before continuing. "My friend Rachel wanted to test the waters and disobey and she went in the ocean. She didn't make it and no one could save her because it hurt to even touch her."

I gulped loudly and he smiled. "Don't worry. Someone would save you because you seem pretty important. Everyone talked about there being a savior and you are finally here. They won't let you die." He reassured me.

"Waiting for me, why?" I asked eagerly.

"I have no idea but we have all known for a long time that a savior was coming and here you are." I didn't speak for a while. I didn't know what I was meant to do or how I was a savior. We continued our journey across the bridge. It was up high so the mist only stung my eyes and as it turned out, my arms burned a bit.

"What can I do for you?" he said softly.

"First, what is your name?" I asked.

"My name is Theo. What is yours?"

"Well, Theo. I just discovered that my name is Lena. I can't remember how I got here or where I came from. I only remember waking up here." I told him confused.

"That wasn't really how it was for me. I am sorry about that. Lena let me tell you what this is." I stopped in place and looked at him. "We were killed." He said in all seriousness.

"Uh." I hesitated. "Theo, that green's gotten to your head. We are standing right here."

"Ma'am." He bowed a little as if to apologize for his silliness. I was faintly reminded of my target. I felt a sting in my stomach but he didn't seem to notice my discomfort as he continued. "You were chosen. There is a reason that we can't talk to our targets. We are dead. We have a master. Dr. Ravana is our master. The men and women we get are coming with us because they have died and are stuck in a limbo. We get them out. We are the protectors, remember hearing that?" I remembered.

I was confused. I just spoke to one and he just saw me. He looked at me first. "But I know they see us. I have seen them see us Theo." I said cautiously as possible.

"Well, they see us when we are allowed to present ourselves. Like last night, I finally was allowed to show myself to my targets. I had followed them for weeks and they hadn't seen me. I know you got the number one target but I had pretty important targets." He told me with a grin.

I smiled. I didn't brag that I was new to this and had the number one target. "How did you present yourself?" I said.

"Uh, Dr. Ravana activates it. I don't do anything. He just warns me before they can see me." I nodded and he put his hands on my shoulder. "Relax, you'll do great. No one will mess with you and when the time comes you can present yourself and kill them."

"Did you kill your target last night?" I asked enthused.

"Well, it was two targets. And no. They got away. Nasty smart little suckers. They are evil and I will kill them." he was enraged but calmed down quickly. "Don't worry about it. You're safe here and you are important to the whole situation. You won't screw up." he stopped for a second and turned to me. "Dr. Ravana is our leader. He wouldn't have trusted you with something so serious if he didn't know you were capable of it."

"Are you sure?" I asked Theo suspiciously.

"Look around you. This is our heaven. We are in the middle of nowhere. We have been given powers, humans only dream of." I agreed we weren't humans, but I knew in my heart, I was no angel.

# Chapter Six: The Stakes

I WAS IN awe as I looked out on the ocean. There was no land around us. You could not see anything, not even a strip of an island. It was our heaven but it couldn't be. I couldn't be dead. I was seen today. Maybe my target could just see ghosts.

I stopped in place. That wasn't the only people who saw me. People, who clearly saw me, attacked me. I didn't mention this to Theo. I felt a chill go down my spine. I was trapped then and people thought I was dead.

"So how did you find yourself here?" I asked curiously.

"Hmm." He paused and talked like he spent a lot of time deciding what to do with his words. "I woke up in a trance. Like you, I didn't remember my name. However, you seem to know nothing about the world you used to live in and I had memories of my family and their betrayal of me. I heard voices and they called for me to do the right thing. I didn't know what the right thing was until I was called to a meeting by Dr. Ravana. He told us that we were a part of a bigger picture. At the time, there were only fifteen members. By the course of three weeks, we were in the thousands. I knew that I would do great things." He smiled brightly. "I was finally home and I didn't remember who I was. I don't know if Theo is even my real name. I was just given this name by my friend, May. She told me I reminded her of a Theodore and it stuck. She is the one who died my hair green. Even though she is gone, I still keep it green."

I was amazed at the similarities of our story. I told him this. "I woke up not knowing who I was or what I was meant to do until I heard voices. They talk to me even now. Faintly but all at once, they scream for me and I know what to do." I told him and he listened intently, hanging onto every word.

"It seems like we are the real angels and protectors. Some don't think so." His face darkened and contorted in pain. "Some are here and act as if they were devils. I hear of torture and punishment that go on when they reach their targets. I don't know why they do that to them. Maybe they are punishing the criminals of the world." He tells me but I doubted it. The anger I felt showed me that I was a monster. I didn't tell him this.

"Do you ever feel super angry?" I said to him and hoped that if he said no, that he wouldn't question why I asked.

"Always." He told me simply. "It is so odd. I feel like I am the protector but I feel wrapped up in anger a lot. And I feel like I am not my own person but instead controlled by something or someone, which would explain the voices." I nodded because I didn't feel like I was working on my own.

"And the powers we have. I can't explain them. I don't know what we are. So I hold onto the idea of us being angels." He turned away from me. I looked out into the ocean as his voice picked up. It sounded as if an angel was really speaking to me. "But angels aren't angry. Are they?" I didn't respond and he sighed deeply.

"My friend May was my best friend. She was beautiful. I loved her. I really did. We understood one another. Dr. Ravana sent her out on a task and I never saw her again. Do you want to know why?" he hesitated and turned to me. "She let her target go. She set him free. He told us. And you know what she said when she let him go? She said "He did nothing wrong. I heard and saw the truth of Dr. Ravana, and this target should be set free." She was killed the next day. Dr. Ravana wouldn't allow her into the compound. I wanted to help, but I couldn't because I would have been destroyed too." He hung his head in silence. "There isn't a day, I don't regret not letting her up; not letting her just stay with me. We could have escaped."

I didn't know him well, but I put my hand on his shoulder. "I am so sorry, I don't know what to say."

"I told you this story so that I could tell you to be smart. Watch your back. I know you are the savior and all, but I have to say this, you're new and I can't help but think he has a trick up his sleeve." I stopped and looked to him suspiciously.

"What do you mean?"

"I trust you. I'm not sure why, but I do. Listen to your heart, I promise it's still with you" I instantly held my hand to my heart. I tried to listen to its beat. I couldn't help but think I felt some rhythm still there. "I don't trust Dr. Ravana, he killed May like it was nothing. Please be careful." Chills ran up my arms as I listened to his warning. "Please don't tell the others what I have said. It was nice to finally let that out. You seem very trustworthy. Hopefully I wasn't foolish to let you in."

"Thanks for talking with me and letting me in." I told him honestly. "I haven't had a chance to get to know anyone." He smiled weakly. "What you have told me means a lot to me. I will take heed to your warning."

"Well, now you do know someone. We should get in there. Class will begin. It's so exciting because you will have your first class with us. You can sit next to me." He backed away slowly as if nothing had just happened and began walking back towards the building. As we entered the hallway, we both shut down. I was frightened that someone had heard our exchange and we were somehow being punished. I caught a glimpse of Theo. My fear was shadowed on his face. Then it went fuzzy.

Suddenly voices rang in my ears, and I knew we were both shutting down together again. I knew because we seemed to be connected. One moment we were staring at each other, both thinking that someone had heard us talking out of line, and the next moment there was darkness. I felt the wind in my ears and knew we were flying away, towards a new meeting.

As we reached the room, I could see and we parted. I didn't know where Theo went but I knew where I should stand. I was in the same place as before, as if we were assigned a space to stand. Dr. Ravana stood before us. There were shouts throughout the entire building.

"Settle down. We are all here." He said in a lazy way as he waved his hand back and forth. We all were silenced by some unspoken spell. I tried to open my mouth but it was as if it were glued shut.

"We must get along with business. There is some terrible news that I would like everyone to see." He told us calmly but I felt panicked. The images before us were excruciating. People screamed in all directions as men and women were seen sawing their own flesh to rid themselves of the horrible disease that plagued the world before us. I was so frightened and wanted to stop seeing these images but I couldn't. I didn't control what I was seeing. The humans were dying. It was our jobs to make them better.

"I would like everyone to find one human in this condition and bring them here to live among us and I will equip them with the gifts to bring others to safety. I will assign you each a target to go and receive but I must warn you." He paused for effect. "These humans are hurt. They are beyond hurt. Each time they amputate an affected area, it grows with double the strength to a new area. This disease is so deadly and so masterfully created, that it was made to be indestructible. No one knows how to destroy it but me."

"I have created the cure that you all possess. This means that you at one point in time possessed the deadly disease of Dermadecatis. You all have been under the impression that you are in heaven but let me tell you, we are the saviors and we are not in heaven. We are the heaven on earth. That is the only way to describe it. The cure for this disease kills people eventually and what is amazing is that death is inevitable when we are given this disease."

He looked down in a wretched way, but perked up quickly. What did he mean? We would all die from the cure we were given already. "But," he threw up his hand for dramatic effect. "There is a true cure and it will be brought to the surface. It is also your job to discover the true cure. It is hidden deep within someone. It may even be a human." His eyes danced across the crowd until they flickered to me and I glanced up in his eyes in amazement. I didn't know anything about this cure.

"The true antidote is able to cure the disease and destroy the effects of the cure that I have created. Whoever finds the real cure will be provided endless gifts and power. I can guarantee that. With a true cure, we can rule the world." He laughed delicately and I didn't know how I felt about this. The world seemed to be so distant from where I stood over the ocean in this house. "Do not let me down. You start searching for these sick humans as soon as you can." He sounded out each word as if they were a menacing threat. His eyes never left mine.

***

We had class. Whatever the heck that meant. I followed Theo into the room. It reminded me of any old classroom except in the far back, was a place that looked like a workout room. There were many machines, including a long tunnel, as well as a huge mat.

"So, this is our teacher, Dr. Matthews. We work on hand-eye coordination in the back. We have to fight each other but don't worry, they'll take it easy on you since it's the first day." Theo sounded more excited than I had ever heard him so I just nodded to reassure him.

"Like I would take it easy on her. That's a big joke." A very tall girl with long blonde hair scoffed at me. "If she is supposedly the savior then why should I take it easy?"

Anger built in my chest. I took a step forward but Theo blocked me with his body, practically shoving me behind him. "Look, I am just showing her around. Give it a rest. You don't have to act tough all the time." Theo said as the tall girl stared.

"I don't have time for this. This girl isn't May. You can't make up for what happened by helping out some whinny, bitch girl." I shook all over with rage but Theo jumped ahead and took his hand ready to slap her. He reached up and grabbed his hand with his other and shook his head all over as if he would cry.

"How about we keep May out of this?" There was a crowd of our classmates all around and I shuddered at the attention.

"You think I don't know what you did to May? You turned her in, I know you did." The rude girl said and Theo lurched forward but then a man stepped in between them.

"That's enough, Cynthia." Our teacher Dr. Matthews spoke with a calm voice. "Get to your seats." They all walked to their seats and I was frozen in place.

"Ah. Lena, hello." He said and I looked at him with curious eyes. "Take a seat anywhere you'd like." He made his way to the front of the room and I glanced over the room. There was not a seat near Theo and thankfully nowhere near Cynthia. I strode down the aisle and finally found a seat behind a girl with jet-black hair. She was staring down at her desk with a death filled stare.

I flopped down in the seat. As soon as my butt hit the seat, Dr. Matthews began to speak. I scowled because I didn't have paper. I had none at all. That was when the girl with jet-black hair turned to me. Her eyes were black as night and I was so captivated by them that I didn't know what she was doing. She turned swiftly around and when I looked back down at my desk, there was a sheet of paper with a pen on top of it.

I didn't know what to do. I didn't say "thank you" like I should have. I was stunned. It was as if she read my mind.

*Prospect*

# Chapter Seven: Bad Blood

I WENT TO class everyday. Theo's behavior had turned a little shy around me and I didn't understand why. He might have thought that I didn't like him anymore because of Cynthia but he didn't mention it again.

Cynthia still seemed to hate me and I had no idea why she did but I didn't bother to ask. She could have been jealous of me for having the target that everyone seemed to want, but I didn't know.

The girl who sat in front of me, continued to give me paper until finally I asked Theo where I could find some supplies for class. He led me down to a kind of store. Within the store was everything. Blankets, heaters and the most ironic of all, swimsuits.

"So this is like a resort. Sometimes I really think that." I laughed as Theo made an action as if he were a waiter.

"Room service?" he asked me as he batted his eyes. I laughed loudly as many people in the store turned their heads to us with disapproval. "So how do you like it here?"

"Well. I have to admit. I don't like some people. They kind of," I hesitated for a good way to word it, "don't seem to like me here." He nodded.

"Some people are just like that. Cynthia is by far the worst. She hated May."

"Why did she hate May?"

"May had powers that none of us had. She could lift things with her mind. She could murder us all at prom if she wanted to. She could do things faster than us."

"That's insane." I said and realized I would have been jealous, but I totally would have tried to learn.

"So what about the girl I sit in front of?" I asked casually. Theo stopped and searched around the room.

"You mean Clementine?" I frowned because that certainly didn't seem like her name.

"Sure. The girl with black hair, who kind of looks angry all the time." I said with a raised eyebrow.

"Why do you ask about Clementine?"

"I just wanted to know her story. That's all."

"Get down." We squatted behind the aisle of stuffed animals. How cute.

"Clementine was the first to receive the cure. When I say this, I mean she was the first to survive the cure we have." I felt my eyes glazing over. That meant that Dr. Ravana had killed people to get the cure to work.

"She doesn't speak. Ever. But somehow she always seems to be up to date on everything. About two weeks ago, before you came, she put a freaking sign on your door saying, "Stay out. Someone is coming." She even fixed your door. There used to not be a lock on it. She fixed it. She knew you were coming and I have no idea how." I felt chills run down my spine as he stood, never letting his eyes leave mine.

"What does this mean?" I followed him as he led me out the door of the store.

"Wait. I didn't pay for this." I scrambled back in the store and he grabbed my arm with a slight tug.

"Lena we don't have to pay." I looked on with confusion registering on my face. "We pay with our service. It is okay." I nodded but somehow I thought there was more to this place then what meets the eye.

"So, Clementine?"

"Lena. I don't know more than you do. Let's talk about something else. Clementine gives me the creeps." I nodded and listened as he talked about finding some new targets. I half listened, especially when I saw Clementine turn the corner, heading in the direction we were just in.

\*\*\*

When class began Clementine wasn't there yet, which was weird. Today was my first day of physical training. All week long, I was learning about targets and what makes them tick. I learned what I kind of already knew. Every Friday was our day to fight one another.

I was eager to see how I would do. I really wanted to fight Cynthia but she had been paired up with a boy named Wes. He wasn't that intimating. He had bright blue eyes and was even taller than Cynthia but he was very scrawny. That was when the fight irrupted. In our fights, we are allowed to hit one another. Even if they are a girl and you are a boy.

I watched as Cynthia was viciously beaten to a pulp. He lunged for her, toppling her to the ground as he collapsed on her. He landed a punch to her nose. I felt warmth on my leg as I saw Cynthia's blood there. I cringed but I was too captivated to not watch. Cynthia was finally at a breaking point. Flames erupted on Wes's hair. Cynthia was burning him and he jumped up to pat his hair down, but the fire engulfed the rest of his boy. Cynthia stood weakly and blood poured down her face.

"Say you're sorry and I'll release you." Fire didn't hurt me, so I was sure it wasn't hurting him. That was when he fell to the ground and wailed.

"I am sorry. Please."

"Beg again." She smiled and I looked to Wes who was thrashing about. Her fire must hurt.

"Please Cynthia." He was finally out of the flames. Blistered from head to toe he stood. Shaking his head as he cursed in pain.

"Bravo." He held up Cynthia's hand and said, "winner." She smiled brightly as Wes limped to the side, almost toppling over. Our teacher was clapping and soon after everyone was clapping. "Now go and heal yourselves." Each of them ran to a machine. They took turns; Wes went first, as he should have. A green light erupted around him as he stepped into something that looked like a tunnel. When he came out, the blisters around him were gone.

I was so mesmerized that I didn't hear my name being called. I felt a nudge on my side and looked up quickly. "What?"

The class laughed and I searched around the room. "Lena, it is your turn. Your opponent is Clementine." My mind froze as I searched the room. There she was. She prowled forward and I stood in place.

She stood in the center of the mat and waited for me expectantly. I didn't know how to fight. I didn't know how to do anything.

I walked forward and as soon as I was nose to nose with her. Our teacher yelled, "Fight." I was knocked right on my ass in three seconds. Clementine jumped up on top of me and started to punch. I heard my scream before I could stop myself from doing it.

As soon as the scream left my body, Clementine was off me in seconds. She soared across the room and landed into the hut machine. When she stepped out of the machine, her face lit up with anger and she raced back toward me, with animalistic speed.

She grabbed my throat as we soared across the classroom. All my peers moved to the side. I caught sight of Theo, his mouth gapping open. She slammed me against the blackboard and for a second, my vision was blurred.

She let go of my neck, long enough to caress my necklace. I jolted at the feel of her cold hands. That was when a foreign voice entered my mind, *"pretty necklace."* I froze in place. Someone just spoke into my mind and I would bet my life that it was Clementine. My eyes widened and I stared at her as a malicious look entered her expression.

Before I could stop her, she yanked my necklace. She attempted to take the necklace from me but it wouldn't budge. She yanked again with the strength that knocked me to the floor. She got on top of me and began to beat my face with her fist, all while repeatedly trying to yank the necklace from me.

"Stop." I screamed at her as she flew off me again, this time into chairs. I was startled to see that my shouts and yells seemed to have a force behind them. She lunged forward again and grabbed my necklace. She attempted to lift it over my head and I pushed as hard as I could. I spun around and kicked her square in the face. Where'd that come from? When did I learn that?

A voice in my head reentered. *"Give me that necklace now."* It said to me as Clementine stared me down from the ground. She sat up quickly and I backed away as she closed her eyes. My necklace lurched me forward, and I was beside her in an instant.

She grabbed the necklace again and this time I felt the chain quiver as if it would break. I gulped loudly. I didn't know the significance of the necklace but if she wanted it so bad, it had to be important. Letting it go would be a mistake.

My fist landed right in her face and her hands released my necklace. She reached once more, and I felt the chain yank again. I started to talk to myself from within as I closed my eyes. "Don't let her have this. Don't let her take it." I spoke these words as if there were a spell and repeated it over and over again. Fury rushed through me.

That was when the floor began to rumble. I shot my eyes open as the ceiling began to flack off rubble. Desks toppled over and I watched as many students fell from the earthquake like movements. The equipment behind us began to fall and break. Her eyes locked with mine and I heard her in my head. *"Stop this."*

I looked at the ceiling to see concrete slam down on Cynthia. "I'm not doing anything." I shouted to her and she shot forward away from me. Her hands left my necklace. *Oh no.* I watched in slow motion as she bashed her head into the wall behind her. Blood spilled quickly from her and I rushed over. The rumbling stopped as soon as I took a deep breath.

I was shaking so bad. "Help." I shouted to the class. My teacher stood in place as shock registered on him. He snapped for two students to help bring Clementine to the back to be healed. Thank god the healing machine was still standing because the room was halfway destroyed.

I swallowed deeply as he approached me. People cowered down as I gazed at them. Many were helping lift the concrete off Cynthia and raising her up to the machine. I felt like a freak. Dr. Matthews grabbed a hold of my hand, raising it slightly, "Winner." He said softly. It was almost a whisper and I cringed at the silence that followed. No one clapped and if tears were able to fall, they would have been. He let go of my hand quickly.

The class as well as Dr. Matthews left me standing there alone. I hung my head in shame as I saw that no one came over to me. Not even Theo, who avoided eye contact as he rushed to see if Clementine was healed yet.

***

You know the saying, "Let the good in?" I couldn't. I really couldn't. I felt confused and I wanted to be alone for the rest of the day. I couldn't help but feel that Clementine knew something the others didn't. I had to talk to her. She spoke into my head and that was something I couldn't just ignore. What happened when she tried to take my necklace? What did it all mean? I looked down at the necklace and held it with my hands.

What did this necklace mean? I let the thought skip from my mind. I was probably never going to have a friend here again. I could count on Theo never speaking to me.

I walked towards my door and heard many voices. I opened the door slightly to see a crowd of people talking together. I shut my door once more and listened. "Did you see her today? What a freak. Cynthia knows not to bother her now. She tried to kill her and Clem."

"One less freak if she would have killed Clementine."

I swallowed and tried to ignore the bile bubbling in my belly. The unshed tears were building up in my heart since they wouldn't fall from my eyes. I backed away. I didn't want to hear them talking any longer. I sat down on my bed.

I didn't mind being alone that night. No one spoke to me as I left the classroom. Class was dismissed early, no doubt because of me. Being alone seemed like a normal thing for me and I didn't want to let this subtle but aching feeling I had into my chest. All the time, I thought of him. My target. He was so intriguing and I felt like I knew him. Not just in a way that I knew Theo, but I felt like we knew each other in a past life of some type. I wanted to see him again. Just examine him from afar again. I had to.

That was it. I couldn't keep myself restless any longer. All I wanted to do was see him. I could figure out this necklace and Clementine business later. I lifted myself up from the bed and moved to the windows, watching the ocean for a second to clear my mind. The waves crashed over and the sky was the slightest bit of black. It looked as if a storm must be brewing in the heavens.

Before I could doubt myself any longer, I pushed on the glass as it opened. I took flight into the night and let my mind guide me to where he was. I was surprised that as soon as I flew over the water, my eyes were blackened as always. It was as if they didn't want me to see where I actually was.

I reached the same town but moved more cautiously through the trees to not draw attention to myself again and see my unfriendly visitors. The house I had been dreaming of, well daydreaming because I never seemed to sleep, was like my own beacon of hope. I was startled to realize that I had been so lonely because as soon as I landed on top of the house, I felt at home.

Conveniently he was in the exact same house. However, inconveniently he was inside the house today. I couldn't break in. He was observant and would know that I was there. I looked intently at the house, trying to discover a way in. I just wanted to sneak around, maybe find out his name. Maybe his room hung a name as mine once did. I froze at my thoughts.

*How did I know that? I don't remember my old room.* I shook away the thought. It didn't matter; this is who I was now.

Again, I looked toward the house, suddenly being able to see inside, as though I were there. The walls had disappeared. The boy was just beautiful as before. He wore a tight, black shirt, and I could see the curves of his muscles. He was deep in thought and his eyes bored fixedly on the paper in front of him. I looked closely and saw many drawings.

There was a loop around something that looked like the letter R. I didn't understand what the drawings were but there were many funny looking R's all along the paper. I tried to make sense of them but I couldn't.

He let out a sigh and got up from his crouched position. His shoes were the same. They were a black, tarnished pair of combat boots and my heart picked up as I imagined them from beneath a bed. I blinked repeatedly to get the image out of my head and couldn't shake the feeling that it was a memory of some sort.

He tossed the papers to the ground uselessly and paced back and forth before walking away. He was in the same exact clothes that he wore last too.

As he paced through the house, I noticed pictures of a family. I tried to look hard at them but something caught my attention before I could zoom in. I realized he was walking to a stairwell and before I could catch up to him, I saw beds toppled over, furniture on its back and walls with holes in them. He wasn't just throwing papers around; the entire house was a disaster and things were strewn all around. Papers were scattered and he delicately stepped so he wouldn't destroy any of them. An entire bookshelf lay uselessly on its side. Books were scattered throughout the room.

He strode down the hallway and the front door was directly in front of it. As he walked by, he held his hands delicately out and touched the walls. He looked to the left and hesitated. He walked  three steps to the left and stopped himself. He held his hand out to the door but he stopped in midair. His mouth curved down into a frown as if to hold back tears.

I didn't know what he saw but he backed away and entered a new room just a few steps away. There was another large bookshelf, still standing, and he stood atop the chair to reach the top book. The room transformed and I gasped. I clasped my hand over my mouth to remember to stay silent even though I was outside.

This was recognizable in the back of my mind but I saw blackness as I tried to look deep inside my mind as to why I was so accustomed to this view. I tried to view the boy again and my vision finally came back to a room with many computers and a TV high upon the wall.

My view returned and I was shattered to see the boy was upset. Visibly broken down into a million pieces, I couldn't handle this view. The boy slammed his hands down on the giant globe machine in the middle of the room. It spoke angrily to him. "Access Denied." And he began to scream. He furiously shoved the computer beside him over and he kicked at it until it busted.

"Damn it!" he shouted. He sat beside what he had done and put his head in his hands. "Why won't anything work? I know it is in her name." He had a crazed look in his eyes. Maybe he was crazy because he was talking to himself. I wanted to go down and comfort him. I mentally slapped myself because that would never happen and never could happen.

He got up furiously, with his hands on his knees to help him stand, to the globe again and spoke fast. "She has been taken. She was unsuccessful. This system is in my name now." he waited patiently and then screamed in aghast when the computer told him again, "Access denied."

"Why?" he shouted uselessly. He typed furiously again. "Why is my name not on the system?" he slammed his hands down on the globe.

"Because she has not failed." The computer spoke in a sinister way. He froze.

Finally he took a deep gulp. "Yes. She did. I saw it myself." He said uselessly in my opinion. He was talking to a computer.

"When the item I need has returned to me, then she has failed. She has died then." The boy lifted his head up, longing in his eyes and confusion.

"What item?" he said very stricken by the voice. He slammed his hand on the globe when it didn't answer. "Answer me."

"She knows. Not you." He crashed his hands into the globe once more. I was surprised there wasn't a crack in this computer globe from all the slamming he did. He looked like a man on fire but he brought himself up once more. He turned around and began typing again.

"Thanks for your help." He muttered under his breath as well as a few curse words.

That was when a strange realization hit me. This boy was not dying or appearing to die so why was he really a target? Was he trying to destroy us with whatever he was trying to discover? Maybe there was a reason I felt to come here other than my own curiosity. Maybe I was going to figure out an important secret.

He sat down once more beside the broken computer screen and looked over at the screen. He stared at it emotionless for a while. Then he began to laugh, insanely at that. I watched on with confused eyes. What was his deal?

He kneeled down beside the computer he had just furiously broke. He took his hand and punched the screen so that it cracked more. He cackled on as he tugged inside it. He made a sound as if he was wounded but he kept going. Seconds later, his hand came out with blood streaking down it in vicious forms but he seemed to not feel the pain of it anymore.

He pulled out a sheet of paper from the inside of the computer screen. Blood was all around it so it was hard for me to read. He pulled the note completely open. It was long but I caught sight of a few words in it. "Trust him, for me. My Lena." He laughed without humor. He ripped the paper to shreds and threw it in front of him. He got up slowly and sat down in his chair. He laid his head in his hands and I listened to his angry sighs before I finally pulled my eyes away.

# Chapter Eight: Destruction

I LAID MY head down on the cold roof and welcomed the shudder running through my body. The note was addressed to a Lena. Could this Lena possibly be me? I knew nothing about myself. I felt an instant connection to my target, and he knew a Lena.

It had to be a coincidence that I was named Lena and that note was addressed to a Lena. Then I had a frightening thought, what if he knew I was watching? Maybe this man was watching me too and knew I would think this note was to me. After all, I'd been told he was evil. I didn't want to be captured again. I couldn't be. I shouldn't feel a connection to my target. Something wasn't right. In order to achieve my goal, I needed to hate him.

I flew into the night's sky and soared for a while, as I tried to clear my head. I halted in midair as I searched around me. My eyes had been clouded by images of the boy and the note that I didn't realize the world around me.

I landed on a highway with ease, far away from the town. Cars were turned over on their sides. All I could think in my head was, "zombie apocalypse." There wasn't a sign of life on the highway and I ran to the side of the road.

The town was not the only thing full of destruction. I jumped over the railings and as soon as I landed on the other side, everywhere I walked was death. Dead bodies surrounded me as I walked. The stench of rotting skin encircled me. I wanted to help these people, but they were gone. Half their bodies were gone. Some were mangled on the ground dead, others were moaning as they lay dying among the corpses.

A man on the ground moved and I ran over to help him. He screeched at the sight of me. I found to my disgust that his arm was completely rotted off. I held my nose, and fought the urge to gag.

"Let me help you. Please." I said calmly to him. "Who did this to you?" I wanted to cry, but I was no longer allowed that release.

He did not have any legs and he crawled frantically away from me, using what was left of his arms to carry his body far from me. I wanted to reach out for him but I was afraid my newfound strength would hurt him instead of help him. "Get away from me." he squawked in a hoarse voice. How long had he been out here like this?

I still walked forward and before I knew it, he was reaching with his good arm into his pocket, and produced a gun, aiming it at me. "Wait sir, please. I can help you. I can bring you to the Doctor and he can save you."

I didn't know what to do, but before I knew it, I was being shot at. I didn't budge from my place. I didn't even feel the pain; it was just an annoying tug of my skin. I looked down to see that I had been shot in the arm and felt the shot when it landed in my head. It was only as if a pressure were being placed on my head, instead of the deadly pain that I was supposed to experience.

I put my hand up to my forehead where I had been shot and looked down to see my skin already clearing where the bullet hit. He shot at me again and it was as if I were in slow motion. I held up my hand and shouted because it was coming near my chest, my heart. I didn't want my body to have a weak spot and I assumed my heart would be that weak spot. The heart is the easiest place to be tricked or hurt. As the bullet approached me, my body formed a shield. A literal force field was around me and it was as if I were in a bubble. The bullet hit the ground uselessly, and the man up looked in shock. I lowered my hand and lessened my shout as the bubble disappeared.

Out of frustration, I plucked the bullets out before they were in my skin forever as I walked forward again. He was just afraid of me, and I knew I could help him. I had to try. "Please sir. If you're done shooting at me, then let me help you. I know it's very frightening. I was sick like you once. Come with me, and I can help you." I held my hand out for him to grab. I would carry him to the compound. How would I explain this to Dr. Ravana? Oh, just went to admire my target but then came across this fellow. Maybe he would be proud I followed his orders a few days ahead of time.

He looked to me in disgust. I shook at the weight of that look. "I will never be what you are; sick or not." He shouted to me. "Tell your friends, I will never be with them. None of us will go with you." He screamed into the air. "You can tell your Doctor friend to go to hell." I flinched away from him and before I knew it, the gun was being lodged in his mouth.

"No!" I screamed but it was too late. I cringed away as the shot fired. I looked in front of me after a long moment. He was obliterated. I chocked on my spit and knew the tears I needed so badly wouldn't fall, as they never did anymore.

People did not want to become like me, whatever I was. But I want to show them that I wasn't bad. Or was I?

I stood as tall as I could without looking at the man before me; completely destroyed on the ground. I continued to move forward through the destruction. I walked, stunned and wanted nothing more than the tightness in my chest to go away.

I reached down to touch many of the fallen bodies. I noticed that many people were in the same boat as my last friend. They shot themselves in the heads to avoid being sick or what I am, I guess. I wrapped my arms around me as if there was a new coldness to the air.

I reached a woman with her child in her hands. They were both dead, but I still reached to feel her pulse. Her skin was cold to the touch and I shivered away from it. A sickening thought came over me as I felt for their heartbeats.

I stood up uneasily and checked myself for a pulse, as I often did now. Pain made me feel alive and when I couldn't feel even a gunshot, a gunshot that should have killed me, it worried me. I felt the left side of my chest and for the pulse in my wrist. I was shocked to not feel anything. I froze in place and realized that I really was dead. Theo was right when he said we no longer had hearts. That didn't explain why I could feel my heart hammering on a few occasions. I had to keep waiting to see if it would somehow miraculously come. Could I have imagined feeling my heart pound?

I kept my hand waiting for a pulse. I gulped for air and realized that I didn't really need air sometimes. I held my breath. I had to try. I closed my eyes and imagined my target. I imagined his hard jaw and the way he smiled. My eyes shot open. *Woo Nelly where did that come from?* I had never seen him smile before but somehow it seemed real. I felt butterflies and smiled. I knew it would come. I closed my eyes and jumped when I felt a tiny pulse.

He made me alive. I knew he did. I wasn't dead. I just didn't desperately need my heart anymore or air. That was a scary thought because I wanted to be alive with a pulse and a heart. I wanted to love, as I knew I once did. As this mother loved her child, I was sure I loved someone else. Maybe I felt love for my target. I stopped. I was sick. I didn't know this boy and I was completely infatuated over him. I had to stop this now.

After a while, I was exhausted from my feelings for my target and seeing the death all around me. I left the dead humans on the ground and knew that I would have to take a new approach if I wanted to help a human in need. I raised myself in the air and looked below to examine the rest of the world.

I realized as I continued my journey that death wasn't the only destruction. The world was smoldered. As if someone tried to burn down earth in it's entirety, but the job was not done. I couldn't bear to see it. I didn't remember who I was, but I was left with a piece of information that was crucial. Earth never looked like this.

Earth was once green, and it was supposed to be beautiful. There were oceans that I saw outside my window. They were not destroyed. I was thankful for that at least.

Nearby towns still held houses, but I had no clue what left them standing. What had happened here? I needed to ask Theo. I couldn't ask Dr. Ravana, because he probably wouldn't approve of me going out into the world without his permission. Theo warned me of Dr. Ravana and maybe this wouldn't be the best thing to bring up.

I flew further and did not see one speck of green outside. I looked at the night's sky. I knew the sun still shone because I saw it when I first met my target.

Dead bodies were everywhere. Not just near the highway but everywhere I turned. It was as if they all dropped dead and no one was around to bury them. Their limbs were bloodied and black rot was all around the dried blood. To my dismay, I realized people were not outside. No one was attempting to help the dying, and it appeared as if no one was around anymore. The activities of everyday life seemed to be abandoned. Not a single store was open, and I wondered how people ate anymore in these conditions. There was no explanation for the destruction I saw.

I lowered myself down to the houses and peeked inside a few. They were all abandoned. The only humans I had seen were my attackers and my target. I reached a lake and smiled at the familiarity of it.

I sat down on the edge and took off my shoes. I lowered my feet towards the water but as I did, my skin seemed to burn as I swooped down to it. I couldn't touch it. Every single time I did, a force unknown by me held me back. The water made my eyes burn and I stood abruptly to get away from it. I put my shoes back on and rushed away.

I could not touch the water and I was startled to realize that I did not have any bodily urges. I knew there were standards to live such as, drinking and eating but I was not hungry or thirsty. I had spent days without either one and I still didn't need it. I was not human, I knew that but why would water be so out of reach for me?

I had so many questions. A rustling sound behind me disrupted my thoughts. I wasn't frightened, but threw my hands up to protect myself.

I didn't see anyone although I distinctively heard someone. I slowly backed up against a tree, hoping my heels wouldn't step on a twig. I amazed myself as I climbed up

with ease on each branch as if there were an actual ladder.
What was even crazier was that I walked up the tree
backwards so I could face the ground to see my intruder. I
watched from above the ground and was startled to see it
was the boy from the house, my target. He didn't seem to
see me and he brought out a bulky cellphone. The cellphone
triggered a familiar sensation, a memory I couldn't grasp.

Someone answered and his magical voice spoke. I felt
butterflies flurry in my belly. "Gabe, I can't do this. I don't
know what to do." He said in a sad way. Someone
responded and the boy responded once more. "I know I
can't give up. Look around you. Everyone is dying. When
she turned into one of them, everything got worse. It's only
been a month and now." he paused to listen. "It was as if the
disease became airborne Gabe." Aha, my suspicions were
true. "No one is safe. They needed her more than we know.
Sebastian left her all the clues. Only she is able to get into the
system. She owns it."

He didn't speak but nodded as if this Gabe fellow
could see him. "I will keep trying. I just don't know if we
should give up or not. I mean I don't want to but maybe I
can make her better. I could kidnap her." He stopped short
and held the phone from his ears. I tried to listen but it
seemed like there was a block on the phone where I could
not hear. "I get it. Jesus. It was a suggestion. A joke even."
He told Gabe. He closed the phone and sighed darkly.

He turned towards the lake and in that moment, I felt
like him. I was just looking at the lake for answers. He

approached the lake and bent down enough to touch the water. He splashed water on his face and I closed my eyes as I imagined how that must have felt.

Without another moment, he flew into the night and I looked on awe. I decided to follow him because he could fly as well. I flew at a distance and I looked on to see that he had a jetpack. Clever. I didn't need a jetpack so I knew he was human. I wished he were like me because I could have a companion. He seemed a little angry though. I couldn't help but want to laugh.

I was drawn to him. This boy that I didn't know was someone I cared for. My mind continued to go dark around the edges whenever I thought of how much he meant to me. As if static was blocking my memory. I hated that.

I moved to the tree outside the house as he landed inside. He took off the pack as he slammed it onto the ground. He always seemed to be angry and I couldn't help but feel sorry for him. He stiffened for a second and peered up through the hole in the roof as if someone were calling his name, as it closed slowly. He was looking right at me with wistful eyes. I winced. He saw me.

I sank lower in the tree and tried to conceal myself but I knew it was too late because just before the door closed completely, he smiled to himself. I caught the glimpse and I was captivated by how beautiful he really was.

I felt myself open up to the possibility that he knew me and that he knew who I was before this. I jumped onto the roof opposite his house, and used my power to peer inside. He sat down on his bed and threw himself back. He looked tired and he beamed to himself before closing his eyes. I felt myself smile as I heard soft snores erupt from him. They were comforting and I found myself dozing off on the roof I laid on to the sound of snores that made my heart patter a little bit. I knew I had a heart from the one who was trying to deceive me.

# Chapter Nine: Drawing Lines

I WOKE UP with a start and searched my scenery. I was on a roof. Crap. I sat up quickly and realized that I had fallen asleep across from my target's house. I jumped up and peeked inside his bedroom; he was gone.

I peered around the house and was startled to see he wasn't in the house. I began to panic. He had to have seen me on top of the roof. I was here all night. I was so foolish. How could I have let this happen?

That's when I saw him, no I sort of felt him, because I looked exactly where he was, in the backyard of the house. He was foolishly pulling on a rope from the ground in the backyard. What was he doing?

I jumped to my normal tree beside the roof I slept on to get a better view of what he was doing. I landed with ease on the branch. I looked down and mentally slapped myself. What if he were to see me wearing the same thing he saw me in to begin with? I mentally slapped myself once more. Why would I care? I would have to kill him eventually.

Numbness went through me as I remembered that crucial fact.

"Hey you." He yelled to me. I idiotically was out in the open during my senseless bickering in my head. I didn't respond because he could have been talking to anyone. He walked around to see me better and I smiled as easily as I could. "Yeah you in the tree. Do you mind helping me do something?"

I didn't say anything and he laughed as he started making some signs in sign language. I surprisingly knew them. "Hey. I can hear you." I shouted back.

"Well, then come down here." He said with a taunting voice as he smirked back up. I jumped down the two-story house tall tree and landed on my feet with ease.

"Wow." He looked at me in surprise. I looked up at the menacingly tall tree. "How'd you do that?" he said with an easiness that showed me he must know I wasn't normal. He turned quickly and began to stalk back to his task as though he hadn't just seen me jump from such a tall height.

I didn't reply but he still led me to the backyard rope. "What is your name?" he asked as he turned his head slightly to the side, and I detected a smile in his tone.

"Uh. Lena." I said silently. I knew this wasn't allowed. Theo made it clear that it was against the rules but I didn't care. I could lure him in and then sneak attack, then eventually kill him. I decided that was the reason for this, and I was going to stick with it.

He didn't talk anymore as he led the way. I didn't ask his name because I didn't want to get anymore attached than I already was.

"Well, Lena." A slight grin played on his lips as he spoke my name and I couldn't help the butterflies from wavering up. "Count of three, pull as hard as you can." I smiled and cracked my knuckles as if to say, *"I can totally handle this."*

"Easy." I said and he squinted his eyes up at me.

He counted, "One. Two. Three." He grunted a little on the three and I pulled hard, well, a little too hard. I heard a crack going along the grass until it reached the house and I smiled as bashfully as I could. "Too hard?" I asked coyly. Was this my idea of flirting? Mental slap number three.

"Actually. It was just right. As long as the house doesn't fall over." he laughed, and I looked up in amazement. Any time I imagined this boy's laugh, it was always this way. It was so accurate. Surprised at myself, I dropped the rope and backed away.

His eyes turned up in confusion. "Is everything okay?" he said concerned. I shook my head like an idiot and cleared my throat.

"I uh.." I stopped myself. "I have to get home. Uh you're welcome with whatever I did." I backed away and took off running as fast as I could. I heard him shouting my name but I couldn't turn back. It turned out I could run pretty fast. When I knew I was out of sight, I flew into the air and away from this place and away from the boy who frightened me with his familiarity.

***

From that day on, I knew I would have to try harder at not letting the boy in or let the mysterious boy see me when I went to watch. I had gone once more to see him and all he did was wave. I cursed myself because I wasn't doing well. I knew I wouldn't tell anyone about this but that was until Dr. Ravana called me to his office on a cloudy Tuesday. He literally called me through the loud speaker and I shuttered at the embarrassment I felt. I bet Clementine loved that.

Aiden came to pick me up from my room to my dismay and disappointment. "How are we doing today miss?" he asked me with disapproving eyes. That wasn't the right word, but he didn't look too pleased with me. We began walking down the hallway.

"A little bored. I'll survive though."

"Yes you will. Say, would you like to go see a movie with me sometime? We have a home theater here. It's downstairs."

I stopped my pace and looked at him with confusion registering plain on my face. "I don't know Aiden." I turned away from him and towards the door. "I think it wouldn't be the best move for me right now." I smiled as kindly as I could. "I have to think of my target." I paused because I felt that I had said too much. An aching in my heart made me think of my target.

Aiden nodded as if he really understood. "That's okay." He looked vaguely disappointed. "Hey! I have an idea. I can help you with your target, I can track them down with you."

"I want to prove my worth on my own." I stopped myself fast, "I hope you understand. I want to do this on my own." His smile faltered only to pick up once more.

"Just a thought." He winked at me and I cringed a little inside. "Ah, here we are." We approached the double doors, and I felt nervousness throughout my body.

He brought me into the room and I was a little shaken. Dr. Ravana was someone I didn't want to displease.

"Ah. Hello." Dr. Ravana said when he saw me. He did not smile but instead gave a smug smirk.

"Hello sir." I said as calmly as possible and took a seat in front of him. He sat behind his desk and glanced over to Aiden.

"Give me and the lovely lady some time, will you Aiden?" He told him with cautious eyes. I turned to watch Aiden go and took a gulp. I was nervous. What if he had seen what I had done? I talked to the enemy and even showed him my strength.

"Lena." He said with sincerity. I was happy to know my name now and was even happier to hear the Doctor use it. "First off, I heard what happened with Clementine." He shook his head lightly, while making a sound of disapproval. I cringed at how cliché that seemed. "Second is a little more important." He hesitated and I held my breath.

"Well, I wanted to know how the target is coming along. Have you found out anything useful about him?" he asked me and leaned in so that he could see me square on.

I felt like blushing but I knew I could hold it in. And I did. Nothing can compare to when you can hide your feelings. I decided to go with half-truths instead of flat out lying. Something inside me told me that I had to lie to not get hurt.

"This target is very secretive." I told Dr. Ravana. I stopped and he leaned in closer. I wanted to protect this boy. I didn't care what he had done. I didn't care if he had really given me the disease because he led me to get these powers. He also gave me hope. "Dr. Ravana, I can not find anything wrong with his behavior." I was still worried that I didn't hate this boy.

He got up and sat down right beside me. He reached for my hand. I wanted to jerk it away. I felt a weird sensation of resentment to him but I left it there. "This target has caused us this great pain and suffering. Have you ever wandered around to see death around you? Well this target is responsible for the entire thing." He smiled miserably at me. "You have been given a great target. He is our number one because he caused the great disease that almost wiped out mankind." I didn't want to face that such a lovely person caused pain.

"Did he really do this?" I felt shocked as soon as the words slipped out and I knew my face showed this. Dr. Ravana's face darkened.

"Lena, this man is full of trickery. He is deceitful and what are all deceitful people known for? They looked beautiful. They are tricksters." He got up and placed both hands on the arms of the chair I sat in. I cringed but moved forward again. I was no coward. We were almost nose-to-nose. "Have you seen anything? Do not protect him." He peered his bloodshot eyes into mine. I didn't trust them like I trusted the beautiful boy's eyes.

"No." I said confidently. I was lying to my protector, my master and my ruler. He didn't move an inch and I stayed put too. I didn't dare to look away.

"Do not lie to me. It will be a big mistake. Even for you." I didn't budge. I felt stronger; I felt defiant.

"Why would I protect our enemy?" I said coolly.

"My sentiments exactly." He moved away from me and I felt a sickness wash over me. I was lying to my creator. "Well, you must find something out for me. What he knows and then you must kill him." I felt my breath take. I dreaded this day and I didn't think it would be this soon. "Do not return to this office unless he is dead in three days. You have three days."

I was glued to the seat. He noticed. "I know, sweetie. It is your first kill. It will be okay." I stopped again.

"I thought we helped others. We brought them to you." I said calmly.

"Oh. You're right." He looked thoughtfully. "New conditions. Three days to bring him to me. Alive. You can do whatever you want to him. If you kill him then that is okay. But I would like to torture him if I can." I cringed again.

"We aren't going to make him one of us? I thought that was what our targets were for." I said steadily as I could muster.

"Not this one. He will die. And you will be the one to deliver him. Fail me and I will show you no mercy." I felt anger inside me. This "great creator" of mine was nothing but an asshole.

I stood up and wanted to tell him that I wouldn't bring my target to him. Instead, I instantly couldn't see anymore. I heard voices. They hissed at me, and I couldn't escape them. I felt a hand close around my neck and Dr. Ravana spoke close to my ear.

"Dear Lena. Do not be a fool. You are so useful and especially for this. He cannot deny your beauty. He would follow you anywhere. He loves you so." I was shocked. He didn't know me nor did he love me. I wanted to ask what he meant by that, but my vision returned to me and I didn't want to push him further.

Dr. Ravana released me, and I backed away from him, taking a deep breath. "Now get out of here. Find him. Do not speak to him. Do not let him trick you. Remember, he is like a fox and a trickster. Don't be a fool." I turned swiftly and knew I would have to capture my target tonight. My feet moved as fast as they would allow me to. Away from his stare. Away from his threats. Away from it all.

# Chapter Ten: Cut Deep

AS SOON AS I escaped through the night, I didn't know how I felt. I wasn't in control of my own body and I wanted to scream but my mouth was always somehow glued shut when I was blinded by an unknown source. It wasn't normal. I hated that Dr. Ravana was in control of me all the time. I wanted to be free of him. I didn't want to kill my target at all.

I was worried that I would run into a wall or worse, get burned by the water. I felt the water singeing me, and I was breathless as I fought through it. I jerked my head around as fast as I could but I still couldn't see. I yanked open my mouth to let out a shout and finally my mouth obeyed open. I screamed and saw that my sight came back, but fuzzy. As soon as my scream faded, my eyes went black. The next scream was long and drawn out, I saw without any fuzz around the edges.

I felt like a bat. They had to make a sound to be able to guide them. I needed to scream to see. I felt my voice cracking as I screamed. I understood why I was blinded. I was being led straight to my target's house. My vision was red and on the side of my vision, I saw words. Before I could make them out, my voice faltered and I groaned in frustration. This was the only way to stay in control and it was flawed by my voice being too weak. I remembered that my scream had affected more than just my vision. During my fight with Clementine, I almost killed her. Or maybe it wasn't my voice because that would have been silly.

I landed on pavement and saw without having to scream. I winced as I saw my target's house. I didn't even know his name, and I would have to kill him. I couldn't handle how I felt. He was so special to me, and I didn't even know him. Dr. Ravana said this boy loved me. It might have been a slip up, but I couldn't help but believe it.

How would I catch him? He would know I was here, as he always seemed to. I needed a plan. I could go through the front door but he seemed so attentive that I knew I would have to catch him off guard somehow.

I stood there for a second before jumping on the roof. I landed with a thud and quickly flattened myself down on the roof so that no one would see me. I slowed my breathing. My hands began to shake from nerves, and I needed a way to calm down. I reached out of instinct down to my neck and froze when I felt something there. My necklace, the one Clementine so desperately wanted.

Warmth ran through my body and I suddenly felt calm. I peered down to see a golden key necklace around my neck. It was beautiful; there were diamonds that followed the side of the key. They each held a promise to me, a promise that I wasn't alone. At that moment, a flash of an auditorium entered my mind. A face so familiar came into view. I jumped up as I felt a memory sweep into my brain and I clenched my fist as it went away too quickly. It was there on the tip of my brain but I could not grasp it. Frustration shot through me, and I felt tears wanting to gather in my eyes but they wouldn't come. I wanted to remember what more there was to my life before this. This key, this necklace was a part of me. I knew it was. What could Clementine possibly want with this? I had to know. But first, I had to do my job.

I peeled my eyes away from my necklace and looked at the tin on the roof. Dr. Ravana deliberately made me land on my target's house so I could get the job done, but I wasn't ready. I felt so close to the house and the boy inside. I knew he was something to me. I had to just ask.

I looked to my side to see the window on top of the roof, the one he saw me in just nights before, was open. I decided I would just have to go inside and get this over with. I swooped down the hole and before I knew it, I was face to face with him. His eyes were striking. They seemed to hold the world within them because I could not move from that place.

He exhaled loudly and closed his eyes briefly. He held a bag that was the size of a bowling ball and I met his eyes as they opened once more. I stopped as my throat constricted. Now that he was right in front of me, I remembered that he was someone I had seen before. Not just a few days ago, but someone I was once supposed to stop. I froze as I remembered he was my target once before.

I thought my life started when I woke up to this new world, but I was like this before. I might not remember anything but his face made me remember something terrible. We had to fly to their safe house. All of us together and seeing him, I remembered it now. I remembered how he made me feel then too. He confused me. I loved him and I didn't know why. My memory must have been wiped because the love I felt. I closed my eyes. I let myself be vulnerable. I felt safe in his wake.

I had blacked out this event and probably many other things until I saw his face again. Then I remembered my mission and this consumed my thoughts. I was not going to be punished with memory loss again because I had failed to get this target once more and had loved him.

He reached for my waist and his face neared me. He was going to kiss me and I felt pure panic coursing through my veins. If I let him, then that would mean I was failing Dr. Ravana. I wanted to feel his lips as his eyes closed and his mouth opened slightly. This was to my advantage and I lunged back. My hand met his nose, and I felt the delicious crack and his defied groan. He was unsteady for a moment but gained his balance with perfect precision.

He lifted his hand to his nose and looked at me in surprise. I watched a small pool of blood run from his nose. For some odd reason, he seemed to smile at me. He stared at me and I was frozen in place by the intensity of this look. Finally, he broke his gaze and I could breath again.

He hurled the small bag at me, it made me hunch over from the intensity of the throw and he took off running. I flew after him and landed right in front of him. I smiled at him villainously and kicked him hard in the gut. He was huddled over, but he stood standing and did not fall to the ground. He glanced up to me, and I saw that blood was pouring from his nose, but he still looked like something from a dream. I was getting annoyed with myself. I shouldn't be infatuated with this monster. I wanted to knock him unconscious so that he could be taken in.

"Lena." He said in the softest way. It made me stop as my heart ached, and I wanted to reach out to him but stopped myself. "Look at me. Remember me." I didn't know what he meant but it slowed me down. He smiled deeply, and I shuttered. He was tricking me.

I threw another punch towards his jaw but this time he dodged it. I grunted in frustration. "Fight back, you coward." I said forcefully.

He smiled weakly. "I would never lay a hand on you. Even here. Even now." I stopped again and shook my head to get him out of my thoughts.

"I have to take you in. You have done an injustice to the world. Look around you and see the destruction you have caused the world. You're a monster. Hit me. It wouldn't hurt. You're a disgusting creature who has thrust upon us so much devastation. It is my job to destroy you or bring you to be destroyed." I didn't even believe my words, it was as if I were trained to say these things. Hell, maybe I was. He didn't look frightened. He stared obliquely in my direction.

"I do not care. Lena, I do not care. I don't want to be here without you anyways. The real you." He said calmly.

"This is the only me that I know and you don't even know me. So will you go willingly then?" I said to him evenly.

"I do know you." He stepped towards me and reached for my face. I slapped his hand away forcibly, and he didn't even twitch away in pain. He reached with the other hand before I could stop it. His hand might as well have burned me. I closed my eyes and I felt like I was melting beneath his touch. "I know who you are and this isn't it. Remember me. Please just try to love me again." I jerked my head away.

"Who are you? I don't know you."

"You do know me. I know you think of me even now. You follow me around." He smirked with an arrogance I couldn't stand.

"It is my job to follow you. I don't know your name though." He didn't speak as I hoped he would tell me his name so I continued. "I don't know you or what you've done but I do know that you destroyed the world and caused so much heartache." Or so I have been told.

"Do you remember that you are the last hope of the world? Don't be so damn stupid." He shouted and I felt my anger boil. I felt his stare boring into me and I was trying to keep myself above the anger.

"Be careful what you say to me." I said through gritted teeth and heard the fierceness in my voice. He continued on. He was not afraid of me still.

"You don't determine the fate of others. You are a stupid little girl who has some fancy new powers that will never amount to anything. You're a useless girl. You had so much to give."

I felt my eyes begin to go dark around the edges, the anger was getting too much. The lamp beside him burst into flames from my wrath. He stopped quickly and jumped. He touched my arm affectionately, but I swatted him away as he flew against the wall.

"Shut up Jared!" I screamed at the top of my lungs. The floor began to shake as it did when I was angry at Clementine. His face cracked into an enchanting smile in satisfaction, even though the floor might fall through. I wanted to smack that look off his face as I flew through the roof before I could hurt him. I was not useless. I was the determinate of if the disease spread or not. Jared. What a useless person.

I stopped midair. Jared. It was Jared. His name was Jared.

I heard shouting in the air and listened closely. It was Jared. My heart swelled. Why did this mean so much to me? "Meet me where we first met if you can remember. You remembered my name. You can do this."

I didn't remember him but the name Jared was important. I felt my heart open to this mysterious boy. He was someone I wanted to know; someone I already knew; someone I needed to know.

# Chapter Eleven: Where We Met

WHEN I FINALLY arrived home, I had to calm myself down. How did I know him? The night passed on and I wandered the halls aimlessly. I lingered by the window in the main hallway to pass the time. My thoughts were consumed with Jared. He was convinced I knew him and that I knew where we met. I just couldn't find it. I sighed loudly and jumped as Theo approached me.

"Hey." He said quietly.

"Hi." I said quickly back, he looked out the window with me. It was kind of peaceful to be with someone who understands when to be silent too.

"I am actually here to bother you about something kind of important." I frowned. He wasn't going to stay peaceful for long.

"What is it?"

"Well, we have a pretty important class to do." I looked up in disbelief.

"I can't."

"Why not?" When I didn't answer, he sighed. "Clementine is," he hesitated, "Clementine is just nothing to worry about. She is just disturbed. It is going to be okay."

"I almost killed her, I can't go back." He turned so that I could see him clearly in my periphery.

"We have all had a spill with death. You will be next." He grinned and I turned away quickly. "I am kidding. Clementine has almost hurt so many of us, she had it coming."

"She had it coming. How could you even say that? I don't want to be this person. I don't want to hurt anyone. She never did anything to me." I shook my head and he walked to the other side of me.

"Lena, the next class is not going to be physical. We just get to learn. It will be okay. As long as Clementine doesn't stare you down, you'll be fine."

"And if she does stare me down?" I smirked at him.

"Then you're dead."

I froze; I felt the icy cold air around me. Then he laughed and I looked on in complete irritation. "What is so funny?" I scowled.

"Clementine wouldn't hurt a fly come on now."

"Did you forget that Clementine wanted to kill me too?" I shouted and he shushed me. *Not to mention, she spoke into my mind, which is pretty damn scary.*

"Clementine was doing the class as you were when you almost killed her."

I scowled. "Did you see her? She wanted my necklace. Why?"

Theo looked down to my necklace and I felt all kinds of self-consciousness. "I mean, it is a nice necklace, maybe she wanted to sell it?"

"No Theo. It was different." I didn't tell him that she talked through my thoughts because then he probably would have told someone.

"Okay, okay. You win, weirdo. So are you coming to the class or not?"

I huffed in frustration. "Fine. When is it?"

"It is tonight at seven."

"Well, Dr. Ravana made it pretty clear he didn't want me around unless I found my target."

"That is weird. He knew you were here. He told me to come tell you about the class. He is the teacher tonight. Look, you have to come because I think he set up this class for you specifically. Why else would he have sought me out?"

"I don't understand him."

"Look, Dr. Ravana is pretty severe, but he does want us to get our targets."

"Thanks for telling me Theo." I said quietly.

"Don't worry about it. You can sit with me and Naomi tonight." He smiled at me and I looked on with a sad face. Theo walked away and turned back once to wave to me. I smiled back.

I was thankful that he didn't batter me for answers to my sadness. I wanted to be alone, and he was smart enough to know that.

Eventually Theo would want to know things so I repeated in my head how the conversation would go. I knew Theo wouldn't understand the connection I felt with my target, Jared. He wouldn't understand. Though I felt like he wouldn't tell on me, I couldn't take the risk.

I continued to think about what Jared said and I didn't know why I was so concerned. I was going to have to turn him in to Dr. Ravana anyways. My target seemed to want to play tricks with me. He wanted to confuse me and make sure that I was side tracked while he made his escape. I had to get there now and make sure he had not left his place.

I turned fast from the window and jumped when I saw Aiden close to me. I ran straight into him but he had not moved an inch. He held me close to his chest and I wanted to get out of that position as soon as possible. It was a creepy sight to see. "Sorry to have startled you." He said in his cool tone. A shiver ran down my spine, and I shook my head.

"You're okay." He finally let me go and I moved a few steps back. "What can I do for you?" I hoped my voice didn't sound as frightened as I felt.

"Dr. Ravana wants to know if you have found your target. Apparently he and his friends are causing trouble." I didn't reply because I knew for a fact that Jared was not doing anything wrong but sitting in the house, but what did I know?

"I do not know anything about him. I don't know how I am going to do this." I sighed because I truly didn't know how I would capture someone I felt attached to.

"Do you need help? Maybe I can get someone to help you capture him." He asked again like he did last night with sincerely but I felt my blood boil.

"No." I said sternly and cleared my throat when his eyes widened. "I want to prove myself. Alone." He didn't look convinced. "Please, I want to be able to know I can do this." I lied through my teeth. I didn't want to capture him and I didn't want to risk someone finding out.

"Alright sweetie." I felt my eyes amplify. I didn't like being called that. "Take them to school. Show them how it's done." He nodded in approval and turned away, I felt a weird sensation come over me and I froze. *What a lame thing to say to me.* "I know Theo told you about the class. We expect you to be there because this class is for you. It is designed to show you what targets can do and will do to you if you don't kill them or bring them to us fast enough. Dr. Ravana is worried about you. He doesn't think you can handle this." I scowled. "I think you can though." He lifted my chin and I felt an eerie feeling run through me. I nodded slightly, and he let go.

He walked away with his head turned slightly to watch me. I stood in place as he turned the corner, finally dropping my gaze. I slowly turned to walk to my own room.

I didn't know how to take someone to school. I didn't know anything. The only real fight I had was with Clementine and I didn't know what I was even doing. My heart quickened as a memory flowed through my body. It awakened my heart and I knew I had to go right that moment. I knew where I met Jared.

\*\*\*

It was as if my body knew, and my mind tried to hold me back. Every time I pictured the place, my mind would try and block it but I kept fighting it. As I flew over the ocean, I felt my eyes going blank and I tried to scream again. It worked but it would falter as it did before. The only thing that left the memory in my head was because I continued to repeat the words out loud.

My mind worked hard to block out the memory. Fuzziness crowded my mind as I remembered the sight but I refused to lose it. I would remember. I had to.

My eyesight returned as soon as I saw land, and I smiled as I flew through the air. I reached the town where Jared lived and landed softly on the grass. The grass was scorched as everything else was around the town. I was surprised that the building still stood because there were countless bricks fallen from the side. A feeling of happiness ran down to my toes. I walked with ease, careful not to destroy any more land.

I didn't see Jared around but this was the place. I knew it was because it felt so right to be here. The Morgan

High School sign was hung over the main entrance and was hanging by a tiny screw. The lopsided sign looked as if it would fall from the tiniest disturbance. There was no one around, and I couldn't help but wonder if anyone went to school anymore.

I pulled on the front handle and when it wouldn't budge, I stared at the lock. I didn't want to burn it but what else could I do? *There must be another way.* I walked back down the stairs and found a window. I opened it with ease; they must have forgotten to lock everything up.

The hallways were bright neon yellow with deep blue lockers lined against the walls. I laughed at how silly it looked. This was my high school. I knew it because I walked up to a locker by the number of 89D. I opened it as gently as I could and smiled down to see my name carved in the side. "Lena was here." I felt the deep marking with my palm.

My heart did a small patter of fear as I heard footsteps in the hallway. I listened intently but then they faded. I decided to follow them. Before I could follow them, I felt a pull in my heart as I passed a room.

I walked directly into the classroom that made my heart patter ever so slightly. I looked around the room and sat down in the seat nearest to the front and directly in the center of the class. This was it. This room had vital importance to me that I couldn't place.

I could feel the room's effects on me as soon as I sat down. I remembered how much I loved school. How much I loved this school. I used to love sitting in the center because I was able to concentrate solely on school, except that day. I felt my memory finally opening up, inviting me to take a look inside.

*The room was filled with my friends but I didn't want to sit near them because it was English class. I liked this class and sometimes struggled so I knew I would have to sit near the front.*

*I smiled at my friends and moved my way through the crowd at the door. I sat down at the very center seat and watched as Kaley moved her hair from in front of her face when she entered the class and I waved her over. She walked to me and smirked.*

*"Why must we always sit in the middle?" She put her books down and catching the eye of Joseph while giving her award-winning smile. "My goodness. He gets hotter every year." She fanned herself for dramatic effect and moved closer to me and whispered softly. "I am so going to date him this year."*

*I smiled to her and laughed without humor. "Are you not dating someone Ms. Kaley?" She winked to me and smiled mischievously as she made her way to the seat she had chosen. She sat down and looked to her right and stopped in place. I followed her gaze.*

*If I weren't composed, my jaw would have dropped. The boy walking in was amazing. He wore combat boots that made him look tough but in my opinion, his eyes softened him. I had to know his name. Before I had the chance, Kaley jumped up and practically fumbled to him.*

*"Hi." She said smoothly, flipping her hair behind her back, exposing her chest and he just started at her face, unfazed by the view, his square jaw tightening in that moment.*

"Uh. Hi." *He said evenly. He didn't seem to be interested because he quickly moved his gaze down to the paper.*

"You must be new here?" *she asked but I knew him. He was older than us and I had seen him around school once or twice. I didn't know his name but I knew he was great looking. Obviously, he didn't need me to tell him that. He had an arrogance about him that only added to his attractiveness.*

"No." *he said curtly and Kaley shook her head in agreement because she obviously had nothing to say. She was faltering for words but then an idea seemed to pop in her head because she flew her hand up.*

"Oh. I know. Why don't you sit with me over there?" *she said as she bent forward to expose herself even more. He didn't even bother to look up. She scowled in a way only I would pick up on.*

*He began to shake his head but then he looked up and that's when his eyes met mine. I felt warmth go to my face and I knew my face was burning a crimson red. He saw the embarrassment in my face and he smiled to me brightly. It was blinding how gorgeous he was and the smile put such splendor behind it.*

*I caught sight of Kaley grimacing deeply as he stood quickly. He completely bypassed her as he reached the table I sat at. I felt my breathing stop cold.*

"May I sit behind you?" *I couldn't breathe for real this time. When I didn't answer, his face fell.* "Is someone sitting here then?"

"Uh. No one is sitting here." *I said calmly as I possibly could.*

*Kaley's glare followed me as she sized me up. Her mouth was in a straight line as she whispered something foul under her breath as she sat down beside me. She rolled her eyes deeply and whispered to me, "He must be gay if he rejected me." She flipped her hair forward to cover her enormously large breasts, and I couldn't help but feel like laughing. "You'll see." She turned to her friend Katherine as if to say, "this conversation is completely over but not until later." and I was left to sit alone with someone behind me that made my knees weak. There was silence behind me but I could feel his stare. I turned to speak because I felt rude but had to be quiet when the teacher walked in.*

*That was when the class started. The roll was called. When my name was called I said lightly, "here." When the name Jared was called out, I heard the boy behind me speak out. I smiled to myself. I knew his name. For some reason I couldn't hear his last name in my mind.*

*Kaley stared at me the entire time. I felt her glare, and when I glanced over and met her eyes she smiled weakly before looking down at the desk. The teacher, Mr. Bills, passed out a paper to complete, explaining we could have a partner. I looked eagerly to Kaley but she had turned her back to me and was already working with Katherine. I felt my face fall.*

*I felt self-conscious so I quickly laid my head down on my desk to avoid seeing anyone. Before I knew it, a hand tapped my shoulder. I turned to see Jared staring at me hard. I felt butterflies.*

*"Do you want to work together?" I felt a blush come on so I turned my head back to Kaley. She was death staring me and*

*Katherine was in on it. I turned my head back to him quickly. I could feel my face burning.*

*"Sure." I smiled to him.*

*We worked through the worksheet in silence, only asking questions we were unsure about until he spoke up again. "So what do you like to do?" I smiled and told him my favorite thing to do was read.*

*"Well, would you want to maybe have dinner with me tonight at eight? You pick the place." he stopped fast and almost stammered. "Of course, you could bring a book to avoid me if you want."*

*I laughed. "Yes. I would like that." I stopped. "To read right?" he was about to speak when the teacher called time.*

*We turned in our paper and I felt on top of the world. I smiled and didn't even care that Kaley looked even more pissed off.*

*The bell rang telling us class was over. I glanced behind me to tell Jared bye, but he was gone.*

*After class, Kaley gushed to all her friends that the boy who never asked anyone out, asked her best friend out. I couldn't help but blush and gush with her eventually. Even though Kaley was being kind at that moment, I remembered the glares through it all. I knew she was hoping he wouldn't actually date me and it hurt. The number one question I had in my head was why would someone so flawless, want to date someone so flawed?*

The chair I sat in was colder than I remembered. I looked at it and saw many names scribbled into the desk. I gasped as I remembered the woman that tried to hurt me just last week. She was in my memory. She was my friend,

Kaley and now she hated me. I had to remember why she hated me so much that she wanted to set me on fire. Maybe it was because I am what I am now, whatever that may be.

There was a crash behind me. A chair was tipped over and I jumped up. I was prepared to attack. I broke my trance as the chair in the back of the classroom moved.

## Chapter Twelve: Holding My Breath

I TOOK A deep breath after a long silence. I was not afraid though because I knew how much stronger I was than whoever it was. If it were Kaley, I would hurt her before she had the chance this time.

Someone peered around the chair. He held his breath and I saw him relax when he saw I wasn't reacting. I couldn't focus. He threw his hands up and sat lightly down on the wooden chair. It squeaked barely audible. It was Jared.

"How did you know to come here?" he spoke quietly. I didn't reply and he smirked. "I knew you would make it."

"I don't know and I just had a memory of this place." I paused. "I remember you sat behind me and asked me on a date. Did we ever go?"

He made a sickened face. "No we didn't."

"Why?" I said a little sad. I must have never gotten to kiss him. I froze as the thought quickly vanished. I couldn't afford to think that way.

"Well. I had to leave on strict orders from your own father." I froze. I didn't have a father. Dr. Ravana was my father now.

"I didn't have a father." I said sourly.

He shook his head and stood up slowly. He reached me in two strides. "You did. You loved him very much. You had a mother too, a wonderful mother. She took care of you always. Look down." I looked and followed his gaze to the necklace I wore by instinct. "They gave you that. It means a lot to you."

I touched it and felt a surge within it. It felt like a magnet. I remembered how confused I was by the necklace, and now I knew I was connected to it because my family gave it to me. Jared turned away from me but I was transfixed on the necklace. The necklace moved upward to my hands. I jerked back and it followed. I threw it out of my hands. What is this?

Jared didn't notice my discomfort as he continued with his back to me. "You were loved by many people and still are." I didn't know what he meant. I stared at his back intently, and I knew he felt me staring. "You need to know the truth of the world right now. I know you wont believe me because Dr. Ravana can be convincing. I can give you proof if you just come with me. You have all the answers. Your father left them for you." He said and I was struggling to answer.

He looked back at me and smiled. "Come." He said simply and I didn't know why but when he reached out for my hand, I took it.

*\*\*\**

He led me to the house that I had seen him in so many times. It turned out we weren't far from it. We walked down a road and were there. The trees swayed in the wind and it felt like something was changing within the world and within myself as well. The wind picked up and my hair whipped all around. He looked over to me and smiled while he moved my hair from my eyes. I shook all over and it wasn't from the cold wind anymore.

He grabbed my hand and I tried to be calm. I felt a little shaken by the things he had told me so far and I didn't know if I should believe him or not. It was not like Dr. Ravana had hurt me in any way. *Yet.*

"This house is very important. I want you to take everything in that you can." I nodded and he led me inside the house and down a hallway. He turned slowly to a door that was left ajar. We walked in and I realized we were in some sort of lab.

"I leave this open now and it's probably not wise, but the world is crap already and there are no answers in here except for when you are here."

"Me?" I said in shock. "I don't even know where we are." He smiled at me and looked back down the hallway.

"Go to the door to the right. This is your house." I shook my head furiously. This must be a trick.

"My home is where Dr. Ravana is. He told me that you're a liar. Should I believe him?" He just stared at me for a long moment.

"See for yourself." He said finally. I turned on my heel a little frightened to have my back to him but I reached the end of the hall. I almost passed out when I saw that the door read "Lena."

"Did you put this here?" I asked calmly. He didn't answer so I opened the door and let my senses take over. My heart sped up as I glanced at all the lights hanging in my room. They belonged to me and I knew that I had done this. This was my home. I didn't want to believe that Dr. Ravana had lied to me but I had to face it. This was my room. There were books tossed in all directions as well as a journal. I picked it up and held it to my heart. A giant L was on the cover. There were posters of my favorite book quotes. I didn't remember much about myself but I did remember books that touched my heart.

"So this really is my house?" I asked Jared still clutching the journal.

He nodded slowly. His arms were crossed over his chest, making him look more intense. I didn't like the flashes of memories crowding my mind. He stood like this often in my mind.

"Now, may I show you what we are here for?" he said calmly. I nodded, and we went back to the lab. I sat down the journal on the seat beside the door. I wanted to take it with me but decided against it.

We reached the computer that was toppled over, the one I had watched him destroy. I reached the globe system as he stood in front of it. He leaned over it. "This system is yours. Please try it even though you're not yourself."

"What do I even do?" I asked hesitantly.

"That is for you to figure out because I have no idea now."

I closed my eyes and reached the large globe. I touched it out of instinct. I jumped back when a voice spoke out.

"Name please." I looked a little curiously as the strange voice ran out of it.

"I don't know my name. Other than Lena." I said to Jared.

"Tell her that." He said.

"Uh. Dear computer globe." I laughed at myself. "I am Lena, no last name."

"Access Denied." My face fell and I leaned forward pushing my forehead against the glass. I couldn't do anything. My necklace grazed the top of the glass. I didn't know what to believe. A part of me wanted to believe Jared and the other part believed Dr. Ravana already.

I jumped back as the computer spoke up as I leaned away. "Access Granted. Welcome Home." The voice told me. I looked back and Jared clapped his hands together with a huge grin. I could not help but feel happy. He wasn't lying to me; so far at least.

"What next, Mrs. Alona." My heart skipped a beat. Alona. It sounded right to me. That had to be my last name.

"Uh. Show me what to do to save people." I said confidently. Jared gave thumbs up.

"The truth lies in you. Not me." The computer said and I grunted along with Jared.

"Well, I don't know how. Show me what is happening to people. Who is doing this?"

"I need approval by Dr. Alona to respond to these things. Insert approval."

"I don't have approval. This is his daughter." Jared shouted to the machine.

"She has the approval. Do not shout." The computer told us.

"I don't have approval. I barely have any memories Jared." I turned to see his disappointment. "I am sorry. Maybe I am the wrong person." I said sadly.

"No you are the one. I know first hand." He told me.

"I don't know who I am." I muttered darkly. "Is there anything I can reach?" I asked the computer.

"Yes ma'am I will get those files running. And please, call me Polly." The computer told us. I smiled and she seemed to disappear before she spoke again. "The files I have reached have been hacked. Someone else has received them but you are the only one who may understand them. One is a letter from your father." A hologram appeared before us, and I saw a graphic of a note.

It read, "Trust him, Lena." I didn't understand it but I told Polly to continue. Was him Jared or Dr. Ravana?

"The rest are files that describe the disease making plans that your father had. Your father created the disease but not to kill anyone. Dr. Ravana took it to the extreme by giving it to people."

"Polly, that can't be true. Dr. Ravana told us that he was protecting people from the disease." I said confused.

"Yes. That is what he wants you to believe. So you shall. Your mind is not your own anymore. He controls it and he may be watching you now. Beware Lena."

"Wait." I shouted before the system shut down. "Polly, why am I so important?" the question seemed out of place but I asked anyways.

"You are the antidote, Ms. Alona." She hesitated. This computer sure had its own mind. "Maybe not you, but you possess it. You have the true cure because." The sound was cut off. I slammed my hand on the screen.

"What?" I screamed. Before she could respond, the window behind us shattered. Someone slammed something against my head. I screamed in pain and before I could react, I was being drug from the room by my hair. The girl with the burnt hair, Kaley, had returned for me.

## Chapter Thirteen: Trapped

I DIDN'T SEE Jared, as I was being dragged out so I assumed that he was with them and was part of the reason they captured me. *I told you he would betray you.*

Kaley's red hair was the only one I spotted before I was hit in my forehead and was blinded. The crisp air was harsh against my bare arms. I felt my shirt being ripped from my body and I felt the urge to cover myself up. I was thankful I wore my bra as well as a tank top. There were hushed voices as I was led into the night. Before I knew it, I felt cloth being shoved into my mouth. I assumed it was my own shirt, I prayed it was. I wanted to fight them but I felt weak. I didn't know why but when they hit my head, I could barely feel my limbs any longer. I was a zombie walking.

I didn't know what I was going to do. I began to gag a little on my shirt. There were too many things conflicting what I knew. Dr. Ravana was bad and he had manipulated me. Or was Jared?

All my thoughts were muddled in my head. There was my name on the door and the familiar things in my room. Could it really be my home? Was I really the key to curing the world of the disease? I didn't know where I belonged now. I wished that I really had taken my journal. It had secrets of my past life and if they didn't trigger any memories, I would know if Jared was being truthful or not.

As I walked, I tried to think of my past but I didn't see much. All I recalled was his face, and it filled my memory with happiness. I saw myself laughing. I knew I had been sick because there was sickness when I saw myself in a mirror. My forehead was rotten along with my arm. I saw him yelling at me, and I watched myself as an outsider, being carried out by a foreign figure, I couldn't see his face. I was being sent away.

I knew that I was okay now because when I looked at myself in the mirror, I was healthy and beautiful. I was once sick so Dr. Ravana hadn't been lying there. As I stepped, I felt something stick to my shoe. I felt as if I were walking on some mushy ground.

That was when I smelt it. I sniffed burning flesh all around me but I did not know why until my vision returned as well as the pain I felt from the hit to my head. All around me was people in chaos. There was screaming and fatal sounds all around me. I was gaging from the smell and wanted badly to spit the shirt from my mouth. I was being led to a house up a hill. My legs treaded up the hill slowly but I felt a prick on my back as someone stabbed me up the hill. I groaned through the cloth and felt tears trying to reach my eyes.

The people around me were cutting their limbs off. One by one, they took turns sawing at their legs, or their

arms and throwing their rotten limbs into the fire. I heard
their screams as the most repulsive thing happened. As soon
as their limbs were gone, a new one began to grow, more
rotten and sicker than the last one. *Just like Dr. Ravana warned
us.* I shielded my eyes away and took a deep breath; I could
speak just a little now "Help them!" I screamed in a muffled
way to the insolent girl.

"I can't help them. This was their choice. They would
rather be this than something as disgraceful as you." She
spat at me and rolled her eyes. "You choose the easy way
out. The beautiful way out. Look around you. This is death.
This is the real beauty. Embracing their circumstances." I
wanted to spit on her as she shouted in the air.

"What are you talking about?" I asked her again
through my cloth.

"A few weeks after Dr. Ravana showed the chip, you
disappeared. The media fell through. A girl and squat boy
came on the TV all around the world and explained what
was happening. They take dying creatures and destroy their
will. They turn them into you."

I was confused. "Me? What am I? What did I turn
into?"

"A mindless robot." I gasped. I was not a robot.
"Knowing you, you probably went there willingly to be
more significant than me." She sneered, and I felt my eyes
roll. She was such a delusional thing.

I spat my cloth to the ground. Hands tightened
around me to hold me in place. "I don't remember anything

from the past but I don't think I did anything like that." I derided back.

"I know you did. You're sickening. You are a monster now. You held fire and threw it at me." She screamed. "You burned my hair, Lena." I looked to her scorched scalp with happiness now. The left side of her head still held the beautiful red waves but her right side was burnt all the way to the scalp.

"You tried to burn me alive you're the monster!" she slapped my face hard and I felt my head whip to the side. I felt my temper rising but I couldn't move my arms. I was weak and I felt my eyes glaze over as I stared deeply at her. I knew the damage I could do, and I would use it on her. Even in my memory, she didn't seem like a good friend. She began to scream and fell to her knees. I bore my eyes into hers and she rolled on the ground.

The man behind me hit my head before he let me go as I collapsed to the ground. Kaley rolled over and crawled her way to me as she ripped my head up by my hair. "You're a selfish bitch and you have to live with it." Before I could respond to her audacious comments, she reached over and grabbed something red. I saw the brick rise before I could move. I felt the brisk pain before I blacked out.

# Chapter Fourteen: News To Me

I LIFTED MY head wearily off the ground and groaned as I felt the excruciating pain of my wound weigh down my head. It clouded my vision with a red haze, and I laid my head back down. My eyes peeked around to see the world as it was. Aside from the men and women cutting off their limbs, blood spilled everywhere; there were a few others around me, sitting. The building was disgusting. I was laid on a concrete floor. There was dampness everywhere and when I found the strength to search myself, I was covered in redness. Blood. I was covered in blood; half my own, but half of the people before me that died or were dying at this very moment.

The people that sat all around me were watching me with sadness in their eyes. They were like me; I knew it because some of their eyes glowed while we sat. I spotted it out of the corner of my eyes that some seemed furious. There was fire all around me and I knew that their anger was causing it. Some of them had cloths of their clothing in their mouth. Some even held blood and dirt. Each time they scowled, I could hear a creaking in their faces. Maybe Kaley was right. We were robots. I tried to lift my arm but realized an iron rod around my arms and ankles was constricting me from moving.

I closed my eyes slowly to slow my breath and suddenly jerked them back open when someone kicked my leg sharply. I didn't feel pain but I felt the pressure. I glanced up to see Kaley walking past me with a smirk on her face. "No sleeping." She spoke as sinister as she could muster, and I scowled up at her.

She continued on to circle us all again. I had a plan to hit her back and as I sneered, flexing my arm muscles ready to break out, I was jerked by the hair by an unknown person. I felt anger and jumped as I saw a fire begin from across the room. Either I started it, or someone else felt angry. I sat up the best I could through the headache and looked to see the girl beside me nodding her head towards the left. I looked on in confusion and shrugged my shoulders to say *what?* But she had turned away.

I peered down at the chains and heard someone hissing at me to get my attention. I whipped my head up to look to my right but then the hissing came from my left. I poked my head up again to see the girl beside me still moving her head furiously towards a girl with waves of blonde hair glancing at me. She whispered for my heightened ears only. "They have really trapped us. I don't know what they used but we are trapped."

"Can I trust you?" I asked calmly. She nodded and her eyes began to glow. I smiled to her as I showed her my glowing eyes as well. "Do you know what is going on?" I asked quickly.

Kaley saw my lips moving and came over quickly to slap me, my head hitting the concrete wall in the process. I felt my vision blur. "No talking. Or I will have to eliminate you sooner." She screamed this time as she turned to face the crowd of prisoners. "You hear that? I will kill each and every one of you. I can find others to test." She laughed as she turned back to me and it sounded like a shrill. She squatted down and leaned into me. I didn't budge from her and leaned closer to her.

"Kill me then. Try to and I will kill you." I shrieked back. The room stayed silent. No one moved a muscle.

"No one would miss you anyways." She said and smiled in a sick kind of way. I wanted to look away but I didn't. "Pick her up, Holland." She demanded as a new figure had entered the room at her command.

I glanced up and looked into the bright blue eyes of a gorgeous girl. Her face shape was an oval and an unusually thin shape for an oval. She looked as if she hadn't eaten for weeks. She had strawberry blonde hair that reached her back and she swiped a piece from her face as she bent over. She showed her white teeth as she beamed down to me. "Let's go." She yanked me up but before she moved her eyes from mine, she winked.

I felt my body freeze, I knew her. "Holland?" I whispered through a closed mouth quietly.

"Sh." She shushed me quietly. "Where do I take her?" She turned to Kaley with angry eyes once more. Her smile had faded completely. I felt my blood boiling.

Recognition flowed through me. Holland was my friend just as this Kaley girl once was. I thrashed about and felt my face get hot. I screamed as loudly as I could, this girl was a fake, and Holland slapped my face. Hard.

"Shut the hell up." she screamed. I froze and glared at her. I felt the anger coming quickly through me and reaching my eyes but I didn't unleash the pain on her. I wanted her to suffer more than that.

"I hate when they act like this." she spat out to Kaley. I felt the rage inside me and I felt myself release the pain behind my eyes but it was as if there was a shield, blocking herself from me. It caused me pain to not convert my anger onto her like I had on Kaley.

"What are you?" I shrieked. Why couldn't she feel the pain I caused so many others? She smiled down at me and I could have sworn her eyes turned a different color. I blinked quickly and realized they were sapphire once more.

Kaley didn't look up but instead threw a hand up towards a door as if she were bored. I felt a sharp jerk as Holland lurched me by the hair to the room Kaley showed Holland.

Inside I saw a machine. People were standing before it as it reached its claws out. As soon as the claws came into contact with flesh, it jerked itself. Before I knew it, I was watching hands being ripped from people. I watched as legs were ripped off while guards held the prisoners up to the machine. Vomit gathered in my throat and I hunched over as I felt my stomach finally give up. I smelt the fire and watched as each limb was thrown into a pit of fire.

This was my fate, to be torn apart and then thrown into the fire as if I were a worthless piece of clothing. I knew I was afraid but I would die with dignity. "I thought you were my friend." I said angrily to her. I didn't look at her and felt the vomit on my cheek. I cleaned my face furiously with my tank top.

"You remember me?" she asked cautiously. She made a sound as if she were a wounded animal.

"Yes. I remember you and you have betrayed me." I looked down at myself, in shock that I could remember Holland. "Look what you did to me." I felt her grip waver and I took my chance. I grabbed her neck and squeezed as hard as I could.

I watched her become lifeless and felt a sick pleasure in my belly until a hand touched mine. I felt the spark before I had to turn around to see who it was. My shoulder felt numb from the touch that could be only left by him.

"Let her go." It was Jared and he looked at me with concerned eyes. I was, however, unconcerned because I was sick of being treated like dirt by everyone. "We are here to save you. Don't kill her. That is not you." I turned slowly to face Holland, she was turning purple under my grip and I released her. She gasped for air while holding the wall. All of the guards were unfazed by her. They continued to rip apart new people. I realized that I was fourth in line. I shuddered. I would die and Jared helped them do this.

He reached for my hand and I pulled back in a panic. "I knew it. You're going to kill me. Look where I am." I felt the fury build up in me so fast that I couldn't stop it. Just as I couldn't make it stop in the training room. The room began to shake. The guards looked my way and before I could stop myself, four bricks fell upon their heads.

I turned to Jared and his face was afraid. Holland ran to the four people who were just about to be ripped apart. And helped them to their feet as the light beams fell to the ground.

"I love you." I heard him before I felt him. He took my hand in his own and I looked at him with wide eyes. "Stop this. I wont kill you. You can kill me. I don't care. I want to make you better. Let me take this away. Let me try." He told me and I believed him. Either I was the biggest dumbass around, or he really cared for me. He leaned down towards me and I froze.

He searched my eyes for a quick second and I felt my heart race. The room still rumbled. The heart I thought I didn't have, started to pick up speed. I had to capture the moment I knew I was alive. As he pulled away, probably confused by my suddenly worried face, I reached for his face and lifted my lips to his.

At first it was tender and soft. I forgot how to breathe and that was okay because I didn't have to breathe anymore. I felt the kiss grow into something more. His hands ran through my hair and I bit down softly on his lips and felt his intake of breath. I was afraid I hurt him until he tugged back softly. I was so lost in the moment that I forgot where I was. Holland touched my shoulder impatiently. I pulled away from Jared and the rumbling stopped immediately. "We have to go. Now." She extended her hand and I was hesitant but with one look at Jared, I conformed.

She grabbed my hand and gave a reassuring squeeze before looking at Jared with a meaningful glance that I didn't understand.

Before I could squeeze back, she was falling to the ground. She slammed her head across the pavement and blood began to spill. I panicked and reached my hand out but then she was screaming. "Help! Kaley. Lena is escaping." I looked on in disgust. Was she tricking me? I stood up straight as she glanced up at me and winked. Then I was being dragged away from the scene. Kaley's red hair was as red as the fire and she screeched into the air. "Stop!"

Jared gripped my hand tightly and put his hand around my waist. We were lunging into the air but fell quickly. I felt dread raise in my chest because we would be caught. He was panting as he tried once more. A groan left his lips and I stared at him in confusion.

He was shouting in my ear. "Fly! Make us fly, please trust me." As soon as he said the words, I willed myself to fly and we did. Many of the prisoners looked on in awe.

"I don't have many powers." I yelled to him. "Why can't the others like me escape, they have the same powers."

"No they don't." he shook his head with doubt as I realized he was clutching onto me for dear life.

"Are you afraid or something?" I laughed into the night. We weren't far from the building, but no one had followed us out.

"Of course not." He smirked at me and let his grasp soften. "Lena, they don't have your powers because you were meant for this. They weren't."

"I don't understand. They could all burn things with their stares. The only thing I can do is fly, that is it and we all can."

He shook his head lightly. "Did you not just see what you did? You almost caused the building to collapse." I shook my head.

"I can't even control that power."

"It's okay. Gabe made me some weapons and gear to protect us. Also, for the record, I don't think you have tapped into your full potential yet." He looked out into the town. "Stop here. We have to wait until Holland is out of there. Then we are blowing that place up."

"But there are people in there. People I don't want to see get hurt. Although they are like me and people seem to hate that, I can't have them dead. I want to go and save them please." I pleaded with him but he cut his eyes from me.

"We can't risk your safety." I nodded but I would find a way in there.

We soared through the air until I heard the sound of swooshing. I almost stopped to see where the sound came from, but I knew as soon as I heard it by instinct. I picked up my pace as fast as I could to escape them. I let the wind whip through me and move me forth even faster.

Just as I thought I had lost them, I saw an explosion ahead of me. I turned around to see that my friends had new weapons on them. On each of their arms, held a large disk. Each disk held a bomb of some sort, and I felt as if my world were shattering around me.

Before I knew it, many were surrounding me, with pointed arms at me, because I was foolish and slowed down. Many of their eyes glowed and a few talked into their arms. Each person had a finger on his or her button to blow Jared and I up into obliteration. I couldn't help but feel shocked when I saw his green hair over his dark face flowing in the air. Theo was here to kill me.

"Theo." I said softly. He lifted his eyes to mine but they were glowing emerald. He didn't even seem to recognize me.

He prowled menacingly through the air to capture me. I moved my arms up in defense to block Jared and myself. Before I could think, I moved my arms in a pushing motion to push him when he approached us but as I did this, he froze before being flown across the air as if I had actually touched him.

I watched, as many of their faces grew fearful. Some even backed up in the air. I looked down at my hands and saw that they were glowing a golden color. I couldn't help but notice my necklace seemed to be glowing as well. I watched their faces as I swiped my hand to the left and watched as people tumbled through the air to the left. Then I began moving them all to the left or the right so that Jared and I could get through. I began laughing as I took my hand and placed it directly in front of a boy with dark brown hair who fumbled with his bomb on his arm before shooting my hand towards the ground. I watched as he splatted on the ground. He attempted to get up but couldn't. I wasn't sure if he was too stunned or just hurt.

My laugh died down as they all soared away. "How did you do that?" Jared asked curiously.

"No idea." I laughed crazily. Jared's gaze never left my face and I smirked back at him. We flew far enough to see Holland and still be away from them.

We waited on the top of the building across the street. The house looked sinister, I could even hear screams from within the room I almost died in. "Let me go and save my people, please." Jared just shook his head. He had a grip on my arm but I nudged it to the side and took off running. I heard him shouting for me to come back but I couldn't. I dived off the building and landed lightly on the ground. I ran inside the side door but was welcomed by a gun in my face. "We meet again." I knew her voice and I shook with fear.

"Kaley." I said through gritted teeth. The barrel touched my forehead.

"Shoot bitch. I welcome it." I smiled at her and her face screwed up in confusion. "Your bullets don't kill me." I said to her shocked face.

"I've killed plenty of you. With this very gun. Do you mean to tell me that you can survive a gunshot wound? Even if it obliterated your pretty little face?" she smiled and I took a deep gulp. *What if it blew my face off?*

I didn't care. I had to save them. If I were a robot, then I would have metal. I could lose my face if it meant I could save them.

A new voice broke the silence. "Maybe Lena wouldn't die, but I can assure you that you'll die." Her hair was bloody now and she had the gun raised on the back of Kaley's head.

Holland clicked the gun once and Kaley flinched. She tried to turn to face Holland but I grabbed her arm as hard as I could. I heard a faint crunch. *I broke Kaley's arm.* The scream was ear shattering. The power within me was a little frightening.

"Thirty seconds and this building blows to bits with us in it. Or I can shoot you so you feel no more burns. Your choice."

Kaley shivered as she laid her gun slowly to the ground. "Okay, I surrender to death." Holland kicked the gun across the room and looked at me meaningful, *"Get the hell out of this room."*

As soon as Holland ran past me, I followed. That was when I heard Kaley speak up. "She can't die but you can." The gunshot was so deafening, I could almost hear the defeat of us in it. Holland fell to the ground and I screamed. Crimson spilled from her arm. *Only the arm. Thank God.*

"Ten seconds, Lena. Get me out of here." Holland said through gritted teeth. I wanted to kill Kaley. I turned to face her in a flash. But to my horror and dismay, she was gone.

I gave the room a quick lookover but she was nowhere in sight. *I should have killed her already.*

Holland made a half shriek and I remembered we had to get moving. I picked her up in one swift movement and ran. When I felt the night's air on my back, I flew up to where Jared stood on the roof. He was pacing back and forth. "Great choice. No way to get down from this damn building." He shouted to me. He was angry but I didn't care.

Then there was an explosion. I turned slowly and felt a bitter sadness inside me. The entire building was in flames. They were all burning. *No.* No more killing from Kaley and her clan. They were burning as they tried to kill and burn all of my people. *My kind are dead in there too.*

What struck me was how easy Jared and Holland could kill so many people. So many people just like me.

# Chapter Fifteen: Blind

WE LANDED BY a river that was far from the house we just blew up, and I was taking unnecessary big gulps of air. Holland lay limply in my arms. "What do we do?" but Jared was already in motion. He worked quickly.

"Give her something to bite on." I nodded and took my shirt off in a swift motion. Thank god I have a bra. *Shouldn't he give her his shirt? Ugh.*

He looked over to me in shock and quickly cleared his throat. He focused his eyes back to Holland and I smirked at him. *Dream of that.* The way he kissed me, I wondered if he and I ever.. I stopped myself. This wasn't the time or place for unclean thoughts.

"Hold pressure here." He showed me where to hold and I pushed hard. She gasped and he gripped my hand. "Lighter." He grunted and I knew I would be blushing if I could.

He went about patching her up, and I watched him work with awe at his ability to think so quickly. Holland's breath returned to normal. "How did you know how to do that?" I asked softly.

"By yours truly." Holland spoke under her ragged breathing.

"Holland had to teach us all about cleaning wounds and dressing them properly. Especially with so much death and injury in this rotten world. Pun intended." He chuckled and Holland rolled her eyes.

"On the other hand, we were awesome." Jared smiled and looked to me fast.

"Now Lena." He shook his head in disbelief. "I told you it wasn't safe and yet, you go in after people and then come out with Holland shot."

"Not to mention, Kaley escaped."

I stood fast. My arms over my bra. Jared stood fast. He pulled his shirt over his head. He was wearing two shirts. *What is up with boys?* He placed it in my arms. I faced away from him and put his shirt on myself.

I turned back to him embarrassed. "And I gave you my shirt, why?" I rolled my eyes and he laughed.

"For the view, I suppose." I had the urge to hit him but I didn't want to hurt him.

So instead, I ignored his comment and went for my explanation. "First off, Kaley would have escaped either way. She wasn't harmed at all. Second of all, you killed all those people."

"Lena, we killed the Earth Saviors. And also, we were pretty awesome about it."

"What are you so happy about? You just killed people." I said bitterly.

"Lena, they were killing innocent people. Those people were humans once before. Some were dying of disease and others were robots. She was killing more people than we just did."

"We just killed people too. We killed those innocent diseased people too." I glared at him.

"Lena, just give it a rest. We can talk about this later." He turned her back on me and I reached for his wrist.

"We can talk about this now." I said as fearsome as I could manage.

He shook his head and I heard Holland grunt on the ground. She was slowly rising herself up. "Stay right there, Holland." He said loud enough for her to hear.

"Look, I want to know why I couldn't go back and save them?" I shouted through the air. Jared threw up his hands and walked in a circle.

Holland was moving slowly to us. She looked like a zombie with dried up blood all over her arms.

"Oh, what about your beloved?" she said eagerly. Her eyes were piercing into my body. Her body was weak but her eyes were the most alive part on her at the moment.

"What the hell do you mean?" I spat out.

"Jared isn't sick, now is he? If he were to go into that room again, he would have the disease. If he doesn't already." She looked away and spoke angrily. "Jesus Christ. It is always about you, us risking ourselves for you. Well

155

you know what? I am sick of this." She rolled her eyes and threw her good arm up while walking backwards away from me. Jared gripped her wrist to pull her back forward; a ping of jealousy ran through me. I didn't want him to be on her side.

"Lena didn't do anything wrong," *That's more like it.* He turned to face me, "and neither did Holland." *Or not.* I scowled at him and he winced a little at the sight. "Look, we all just have to regroup and talk this out. Okay?" I nodded. "Okay?" he faced Holland and she shrugged her good shoulder. "Now do you forgive one another?" We both nodded and he pulled away. Holland locked eyes with me and I felt pure hatred for her.

"I want to know what you were doing in there?" Holland looked down and I could tell she was about to lie. "Before you lie to me, I think this should be our honesty hour because I am sick of being torn between two things. I just want the truth." I shuddered because I couldn't stand not knowing what was really happening here.

"First off, I wasn't going to lie." She glared at me and then to Jared, who sat down on the ground beside us. "Second off, I was there to save your ass as always. You are always getting us into a mess. From the moment you made it to the-." She stopped because Jared held up his hand as if to wave off something. She hesitated but continued on. "Lena, I was sent here to keep an eye on you because you just don't know what you're actually dealing with." Holland was unsteady and Jared reached up to plant her beside him on the ground.

"What am I dealing with exactly then? I woke up a few days ago remembering nothing. And when I saw Jared's face, I remembered I was supposed to capture him. That is all I have in my brain. Other than how much I love him and my first memory of him ever." I smiled down to him and Holland looked on annoyed.

"That's all very touching, but I want to know how you remember things. Those people that are turned are mindless but with you it seems to be wearing off. Why?" she asked as her eyes glazed over. Jared from the grass glanced up at me.

"I don't agree with that at all. I met a boy named Theo, and he seemed to remember things like I do. I didn't get to talk to much of anyone else because I was busy with my target." I hesitated. "Theo was out there tonight. He seemed to be brainwashed today."

Holland huffed under her breath. "Lena, what do you remember? We really need your insider information." Holland told me and she didn't look as livid as before.

"Well, first off, they are looking for you. Obviously." I said to Jared and he took a big gulp. I turned to Holland to fill her in. "I was given Jared the moment I woke up."

"I know the gist of that. Jared and I do talk all the time." She rolled her eyes and I continued without a moment's reluctance.

"Jared, they want you bad because you have been snooping around or something." Holland momentarily froze. "There is a voice inside my head and my eyes become blurred up. I am guided over an ocean and am given my vision after I reach land."

Holland spoke up louder than I had ever heard her. "Why the hell would they give you Jared? Did they want you to know? This has to be a trap." She said alarmed as she began searching from the ground of the perimeter for signs of life. She laid flat on the ground, wincing, as she crawled between bushes. I felt like laughing but then she spoke again. "Jared, we have to leave." She whispered as she threw a hand to her chest as she rolled over. "They are watching us. Oh my god." Tears spilt down her face and Jared lifted himself up off the ground to her hiding spot.

"Holland. Calm down. What are you talking about?" Jared said in soothing words.

"They know we are here. Oh my god."

"Everything is going to be fine." *Oh god. A feeling came over me.* "Jared," I said through gritted teeth. He glanced over at me and Holland peeked around the bushes. "What time is it?"

"It's past ten why?" It was after seven. I was expected back for my class. The class completely designed to me.

"I think…" I shuddered as Jared walked slowly to me.

That was when a sensation came over me. Voices spoke in my head. They hissed and wheezed their voices at me and I couldn't help but listen. It was in my brain that I had to listen.

I heard a whispering in my head that overshadowed all of the other ones. It shook all through my body. *"Get them Lena. All of the enemies are in front of you. We will find you if you don't. Prove yourself."* It shouted to me. Jared grabbed my waist and I moved away from him as fast as I could. Hurt registered all over his face.

"Go away." I screamed. "They are sending me after you." Jared looked at me with frightened eyes. No one budged. "Leave!" I shouted as loudly as I could. Holland got up as quickly as she could with her damaged arm and touched my shoulder. She looked into my eyes with a meaningful look before she ran. Jared stood in place. His eyes were bulging out of his head but he didn't move. "Please go." I said and I reached out to touch his face.

He pulled his face down to mine and I thought he was going to leave me with a kiss but his lips parted open and he whispered. "I am not leaving you. Not again."

"Jared, no please. They will come and they will get you this time. Please." My last plead was cut short when the blackness came over my eyes.

I opened my mouth to tell him to go once more but I heard a foreign voice coming out of my mouth. "I told you once." I laughed a cruel voice. I felt an inner part of me trying to thrash about and get whatever was inside me to get the hell out. "Now that you didn't obey, you must die." I was trapped; I hoped he knew that this wasn't me. I hoped I was glowing on the outside or something was different to show him it wasn't me. I didn't feel Jared's touch anymore and I hoped he was gone.

These words were not mine and that voice was not mine. I was being taken over, and I knew I would lose myself. My body had a mind of it's own because I reached in front of me and found a neck.

I gripped it as tightly as I could and felt wind rushing all around me. Too many voices told me to stay put and somehow my body obeyed. I heard him struggling, he whimpered under my hold and I felt like crying but I couldn't.

I heard a shout and realized that Holland was behind me again. "Lena. Find yourself. Get strength and let go." I wanted her to be safe and she wasn't. I wanted to claw at my own face but I couldn't bring myself to fight through the blackness. Something was holding me in place.

I felt a wild wind. It brought chills down my back and before I knew it, a rich voice approached me. "Oh Jared. How naïve of you to think you could win." It was Dr. Ravana; he was the main voice in my head always. I wanted to take this anger out on him; the voices told me to stay in place. "Our Lena here is going to kill you if I tell her to. She can do it." I heard the command and felt my hand involuntarily squeezing his neck harder with his accompanying rattles.

"Lena can't think anymore. I gave her some space to let her think willingly and she remembered you. To my disappointment, she betrayed me and now she will be punished for it. But finally, she is mine. She really is mindless and she is in my control. I should have just done this to begin with. But I wanted to see how the mind works. How the mind remembers even when it is almost taken. I gave her powers and abilities and she tried to defy me. Now look at her. She is going to be trapped and blind forever. Thanks to you." He laughed menacingly. I tried hard to release Jared but I could not. "That's okay. I have had help to know all about her and you. I have had help to know how to control her. I know everything about her mind."

Jared struggled to talk and I felt my grip tighten. *"Release him."* Dr. Ravana told me and the power that controlled me let me release him.

He gasped for air and spoke with a voice that was scratchy and raspy. "Lena is still in there. I will bring her out again. You're a liar. You tried to put full control and it worked but she fought through it." Jared shouted to him.

There was silence. "A betrayal runs deep, son." Dr. Ravana's cruel voice told Jared.

"I am no son of yours." Jared said viciously. I could imagine his jaw clenched. I was still eloped in blindness.

"So many have betrayed you. And you will soon find out that you are alone." He said simply. "Take him away." I could imagine him throwing up his hands.

Before I knew it. My hand was eloped around his body and I was walking forward. I didn't know where I was but I knew where I was going.

My head continued to tell me that we were headed to headquarters. I wanted to feel the violent strikes of tears down my face. I wanted to know that I was alive. That I was human. That I was a companion to Jared. If I could cry, that meant I still had some humanity left. I wanted him to know I was here. I would fight. I would not give up and I wouldn't let myself be controlled.

Suddenly, I felt the control on me wavering. The voices in my head were only a murmur now. I had to try to scream at the voices in my head. So I thought as hard as I could, *"You will lose. I will have control of my mind and kill you all."* I shouted and knew I was triumph. I couldn't hear the voices.

All at once, the voices spoke loudly and one screamed over the others, *"That is what you think Lena. You will lose and have lost everything. Say goodbye to your humanity. Say goodbye to Jared. You are under my control now."*

I felt my heart break. Bile raised in my throat. I could remember that voice anywhere. I forgot all about it. All about what brought me here. Hearing that voice, I remembered everything. The voice of the last hope was my enemy now. It wasn't something I could forget.

# PART TWO:
## JARED

### Chapter Sixteen: What I Know Is Useless In Saving Her

NOW WHAT? THAT is all I can manage to comprehend in my mind right now. Lena is being controlled. She was never with my dad. I shouldn't have listened to Gabe when he told me she was on my dad's side. He imprisoned her mind and now she was gone by the looks of it. He just told me. I can't believe I let her get sicker. She shouldn't be here. I didn't know who lied to me, but I knew it wasn't her.

I wanted more than anything to take back those last moments. We fought with one another. Yes, it wasn't that bad but I didn't want it to be the last thing she remembers of me. If she ever remembers anything again.

Lena was squeezing my waist, and I didn't dare move from her grasp because if I did, she might have ripped some skin off. I tried as hard as I could to search her eyes. She only showed the whites of her eyes and they glowed an emerald green that Joseph once had. Sometimes when Lena was watching me from the tree, I could see that glow. When Lena first showed up there, I thought it was the end for me.

To be honest, if Lena would have killed me, I think I would have gone gladly. She was so beautiful. She was always stunning but now she had a glow to her. It was as if they turned up the volume of her beauty. The thing that made her so beautiful to me was the fact that she was somehow still in there. She was somehow still Lena.

We rushed up into the air and for a second, it was just the two of us. I watched below as the waves crashed over huge rocks. I remembered Lena saying that she never got to see this ocean, and I decided I would try to figure out why. The ocean was rough but underneath all those waves, what could there be? That must be what they didn't want her to see.

When we landed on the sand, I looked beside me to see my dad and his posse of four behind him. Each of the four with him looked identical. They all had blonde hair. They each towered over my dad.

Lena shoved me forward, and I was yanked back into reality. I was being led to a long island. A silver and gold glass tower was the only building on the island. It was huge and I wasn't sure how I never saw it until I was on the sand. As we approached the building, the doors slid open. Joseph walked out and bowed down to my father. I snickered only to get his eyes turned to me.

Lena was guiding me and stopped abruptly, bringing me to bang into her chest. She felt like bricks, and I cringed. That would bruise.

"He is waiting for us upstairs." Joseph spoke to Lena. "Take him there." Joseph stayed behind to talk to Dr. Ravana. I froze. Lena treaded on and yanked me from my frozen state.

We walked through the glass door. Lena moved quickly because the breeze picked up some water, spraying us in the arms. To me, it felt wonderful to feel coldness in the warmth outside. It was night, but the humidity was excruciating. To Lena, the water seemed to leave red welts on her body. Then it hit me, they were surrounded by water, even though they could not go near the water or in it. Why were they enclosed around it? Was it to keep them in?

"Welcome." Many voices called to me. I curtly turned my head and saw a crowd surrounding Lena and I. I spotted a boy with green hair looking at Lena intently. Jealousy coursed through me.

"Lena?" he asked calmly, my wariness thickened. He ran to her and touched her arm. I wanted to jerk it away but I couldn't. "What is wrong with her? The last time this happened to someone, they were gone forever." He faced me now and looked like he was in pain. "Help her. Whoever you are." He pleaded with me.

I nodded and was about to speak but that was when I saw Joseph approaching us quickly. The boy was hit in the back of the head with something sharp. I couldn't help it. I ducked away from it. Joseph quickly dragged the green haired boy to the side and laid him against the wall. He slumped over and fell to his side with a thud. We quickly began to walk again and I tried to turn back to him but Lena still prevented any movement from me.

I needed to pay attention to as much detail as I could. I had to remember all the turns I made and all the pictures that connected to each pathway. I cut my eyes to the side to examine the walls and was disappointed to see that each hallway held the same things. The walls were a dark blue and there were no pictures on the walls. There was no way I could decipher from each hallway and I grunted in frustration. I felt a sharp hit to my back and I turned my head to Joseph. He smirked at me and was enjoying that he was finally controlling me. I examined his eyes and noticed that he was not being controlled.

His eyes were not glowing as Lena's were, which meant he worked on his own, evil and all. Every once in a while, his eyes would flicker red. I stared at him in disbelief. Red eyes? The hit to my head must have been messing with me. I turned quickly away from him when he raised his hand as if to hit me again.

The hallways were endless. We turned right then left, then left again and I couldn't keep up. I had to contact Gabe. He was my only hope of finding a way out of here. Just then my heart started to pound all the way up to my ears. I remembered that my phone had not been removed and that was a good thing. I kept my untraceable phone hidden away all the time.

I checked for cameras. Every single hallway had a new camera. The staircase seemed to have a camera at every floor too. There was no way out without being spotted.

After ten flights of stairs, we reached a black door. Lena kicked it open with her foot, careful not to release me. We continued walking a few more turns and then we reached a new black door. It opened without anyone touching it. I stopped and Lena pushed me forward.

Inside held a man pacing back and forth. His pace reminded me of my own pace. It was as if we would never just stay in one place. We couldn't because our minds were running so fast. We tried to pace ourselves on the outside and hoped it would work on the inside somehow. He was looking down and his face was forced in concentration. *Could it really be him?*

He finally looked up with a blank look on his face. He smiled deeply at Lena with pride and I felt rage. His eyes reached my face and his smile turned into a sadistic one.

"Ah. I wondered when I would see you again." I was frozen in place. I couldn't breathe anymore.

"Why are you here?" My voice was barely a whisper. "What are you doing?"

"Yes, I am alive and I have chosen the path that you were too weak to chose." He spoke from across the room but the words pierced my ears as if he were shouting in my ears while standing right next to me.

I couldn't believe my eyes. How could it be?

My brother Aiden stepped before me. "And Lena seems to be under full control. Excellent." He walked forward, right in front of Lena's wide, bright eyes. He caressed her face, and I flinched under her weight. She no longer was pulling at me from my movement. It was as if she were frozen by his touch. I jerked harder to reach him but it was like I was attached to a statue. "Although she was much more fun with her own will." I lunged forward; my goal to knock his hands away, but she held me still.

"Aiden knows a lot about Lena; maybe a little too much. Lena was very willing to get to know Aiden." Dr. Ravana spoke up from behind me, but I couldn't bear to hear it. I felt my body shake with anger.

"I swear if you did anything to her." I screamed. Aiden didn't move his hand but stopped his caressing. "She didn't know what she was doing, and Aiden doesn't know her as I do." I said facing my father. I still defended her grace. I didn't believe a word of it.

"And if I did? What will you do?" Aiden approached me with his forehead almost touching mine.

"I will kill you." I said through clenched teeth. Aiden scowled but backed away.

"You know, you're right. Lena didn't know what she wanted or whom she loved before. You know, I don't think you ever loved her. You wanted to control her and you sent her here to die." He said simply. He crossed his arms over his body.

"I didn't bring her here." I said defensively.

"No, but you told her to come here. We know all about it. Lena's memories became ours as soon as she was sent here. We get everything. It's like we suck all their life out and get all their precious moments. You know what really pissed me off?" I saw Dr. Ravana flinch but he stayed composed. "Lena's memories had a block on them. How very strange. Isn't it?"

My heart quickened. "What do you mean?" I asked calmly. I felt as if my heart was going to explode from pounding so fast.

"The first memory we received was when Lena's family died. How could that be? An insignificant amount with nothing to tell us." Aiden's voice cracked and his exterior features turned up angry.

"Enough." My father's even tone came out jagged. "Enough." He tried once more. "We are giving the enemy the upper hand Aiden."

"Have a given away a secret?" Aiden spoke through clenched teeth. "Father, you have hidden so much from me. Forgive me if I don't know what secrets are too precious to tell."

I didn't have to look at my father to know he was angry because Aiden shrunk into himself and nodded in agreement. The conversation was over. For now.

This was obviously something important, and Aiden didn't have my father's full trust. I would play into that, when the time came that Aiden and I were alone. I knew Aiden. I knew how to make him tick and I would get the truth about her memories. Aiden turned quickly on me as if he were going to pounce.

"Could you not bare to see her die as you couldn't bear to see our mother die?" He mocked me, and I tried my best to stay calm. He started to circle me and I felt his voice pricking my skin with its roughness. "You walked away from her when the going got tough. As you walked away when mother was dying. Father and I haven't forgotten."

"I never left mother's side. What could you possibly be referring to, Aiden? When I took care of you, while father was out making millions; and for what? So he could take care of our mother? She wanted to have people around her. She didn't want to be alone. Money meant nothing to her. So tell me, how did I abandon the family?" I felt my heart swell with memories of my mother. I didn't talk about her ever. She had died when I was younger and I didn't want to relive the images.

He got up into my face once more. "We all know that you killed mother. Not us."

My muscles clenched in response to his words. I didn't kill my mother but it never stopped Aiden from blaming me. It was no use to try to explain to Aiden that it was actually our father who was the monster.

"I think I'll go back to Lena now. You were useless to her and she knew it. We all knew she would die but you couldn't face it, so you ran off to make a safe house, when the real answer was to control the world with your father. As I have done now. What would mother want?"

I laughed half-heartedly. "You will lose." I said cold but I knew in my heart, they kind of already won. I looked to Lena, at my latest failure. She was being controlled and it was me who had to take the blame for it. She stared forward, dragging me on; I knew she couldn't hear anything. I wished she could because she would know the truth about so much.

"Oh, are we going to lose, Jared? We own every single mind in this building. And many more outside of these walls. Lena here was the big test. The final test was to see if a resistant could be fully controlled. We have come to find out that we can fully control without damaging the brain and destroying the body." He laughed cruelly. "Tomorrow, we are going to generate a new way to control all of these people. Those that have been controlled will be given the cure in a new way."

I heard Holland for the first time and jumped at the sound of her voice. "Faith isn't lost; I know we have someone who can stop you." She screamed at the top of her lungs. I knew she meant Gabe. I hoped she wouldn't tell them about him. He was our only secret weapon.

"Ah. He isn't much of a threat anymore." Her jaw clenched and her mouth moved to a solid line. Her eyes widened and I felt mine widen as well. How had they known about Gabe? And how did they know that we meant him at all?

"What the hell do you mean?" she said weakly, her eyes begin to water a little. Then as if she were going into a fire, she was screaming. "Where is he?" She shouted as she thrashed about.

She managed to kick over many things. Her guard grabbed a hold of her, letting her go was a mistake. I found that he wasn't under control either. He began to drag her from the room but she fell to the ground. She hit the side of her face as she dug her nails into the ground. Blood spilt from her splintered hands and tears rushed down her face as she screamed out. The man dragging her released his grip once more and she scrambled towards me. She called my name and I was wide-eyed and afraid.

"Please, Jared. We have to get out of here." She screamed to me but I was locked in place by Lena. In an instant my body convulsed. "Let her go. You fucking idiots." I struggled against Lena but she just held me. I didn't care if I ripped my arm in half. I had to get to her.

The man finally reached her and slammed his foot into her face. I held my breath and stopped moving. She was knocked unconscious and he picked her limp body from the ground. Blood poured from her head and seemed to spill from her ears. I screamed her name over and over again. But the door was slamming behind the man.

Aiden turned to me with a satisfying look on his face. He began to back up towards the door. "Ha. Don't mind me, just taking care of the trash." He smirked to me for a long time.

"Don't touch her. Don't even think about it." He smiled at me as he opened the door to let himself out. I heard things being thrown on the ground. Things were clinging loudly in the hallway, and I cringed at the sounds. "We have big plans for her." He slammed the door.

# Chapter Seventeen: Ready For the Fight

DR. RAVANA AND Joseph stayed behind in the room. They spent most of their time glaring at me and scoffing every time I made a sound. Lena practically rolled over me as she brought me to a large machine.

It was black and chains were sprung from the ceiling. I felt the cold chains as they clamped onto me. As soon as they were on, they bit down into my skin, piercing them. I felt as blood ran down my arms.

The pain didn't stop me from yelling for Holland. Where were they taking her? She was the only person left for me to talk to. The only one left to fight with me. As soon as the chains no longer dug into my skin, I was lifted up into a standing position. My arms fell asleep thanks to being trapped with my arms raised over my head.

Joseph took a step up to me and stared me down. I didn't flinch away until he lunged towards me, finding his hand in my gut. He punched me with a power that wasn't physically possible for a human. Pain writhed through me and I strained out a grunt. "Shut up already. She can't hear you. The room is sound proof. So please, do us all a favor, and shut the hell up."

"You're pretty brave now that I am chained up." I spat back to him.

He walked back to his position of standing with his arms crossed beside my father, ignoring me. It was as if he were as a guard to him. My father coughed softly beside him. I rolled my eyes.

Lena stood beside me, her eyes staring blankly out the window. As I stared down at her, I was alarmed by the fact that she was probably never coming back.

I let out a gasp as my vision begins to darken. There was a sharp pinch that passed through my cheek. I looked over to see the remains of a large needle that was just shot into my cheek. Joseph held it up in triumph and I was suddenly alarmed. *When did he even move?* Was I just injected with the disease?

Before I can manage to comprehend anything, specks cloud my vision. Then there is complete nothingness. I feel my face become moist. I clench my teeth as I realize that I am being spit on. There is laughter. Their cackles fuel my anger but I bite my tongue to keep from lashing out since I am defenseless. I open my mouth and feel something or someone holding my mouth wide open.

I shut my eyes to snap out of my fuzzy vision, but as I try to reopen them, I am startled to realize that my eyes have been glued shut. Suddenly, a new sensation takes over. The taste of metal and some form of acid fill my mouth. Whatever was holding my mouth ajar has been removed and I attempt to spit out the material in my mouth, but it is as if it was gluing my mouth shut. I realize that I couldn't scream even if I wanted to. My mouth was being sealed shut.

I was blessed with the ability to hear, and blessed I was. I heard Lena's screams. In my darkness, I start yanking my arms from their chains, only to feel my skin being ripped a little more. If they were hurting her, I would rip my hands down. That was when I heard her. "Stop it!" she screamed through her shrills.

She was fighting her control. She must still be resisting and a flaw must be in their system. There is a loud sound accompanied by a low screeching sound. She makes no more sounds and I stop moving to listen to the rest of the commotion.

"Joseph!" My father shouted as I jumped in place. He was certainly frightening to hear. "Go and bring him to me. Now." His voice was soft but his words pierced the air. "And you tell him that I need the project done faster because obviously some people are resisting. Tell him if he finishes faster that I can give him his prize much faster. Although, he doesn't deserve it after this outbreak." I listen intently as he sighs deeply. "Joseph, be careful with him. He is a little off balance at times." My father spoke so kindly to Joseph. Maybe he wished that Joseph were his own son.

"I will go tell him." There was a silence and I realized that he must have left the room. All I could hear was typing. The typing was frantic, and I was sure it had to do with Lena. Everything had to do with Lena. I felt someone staring at me. The typing ceased for a second before continuing and I knew my father was alone with me.

I felt something surround me, the claustrophobia I had was taking over, but I could not fight it because I was chained tightly in place. That was when the chains were released from my hands. I felt my arms drop harshly to my side. I felt the tingling in my arms as they tried to wake. I heard footsteps approaching me, and I stiffened in response. My vision was still gone and my mouth was still shut. I was helpless.

Something new started to close me in and I tried to move, but I was somehow trapped still. I stood just listening to my surroundings. There was only silence, and the hairs on my body began to rise because I didn't know what to expect next.

Slowly, my eyesight returned, and I could open my eyes once more. I peered down but as I did, I was restricted. My face was cold and it dawned on me that I couldn't move my head. All around me was cold metal that held my head promptly in place and looking ahead.

From my periphery, I saw that Lena was getting up from the ground. She was beside me once more, dazed and hypnotized as before. This time she was staring at the wall and not out the window in the room. She was fighting it. I had to believe that she was. Each time I glanced over to her, I noticed a curious thing. Her eyes began to flutter furiously every time my eyes bored into her head.

Dr. Ravana snapped me from my discovery as he walked forward holding a book in his hands. "The weak, loner Jared. Ah. At last I can say that I have you caught. I mean look at you. You are helpless. You are worthless. You thought that you could destroy me, as well as the world I have created for myself. You sacrificed so much to lose in the end. How does it feel?" he smiled menacingly, and I moved my jaw and found that my mouth was able to move once more.

"I have not lost. I have many people that will help me." Dr. Ravana just laughed as he tossed his hand in the air to me as if to dismiss the thought.

"We will see. I am leaving the room for a little while." He yanked the door open and I heard screaming that filled the room. Holland was being punished. I couldn't even imagine it. "Try not to move." He winked at me, and I felt my mouth clenching up. He slammed the door shut and the screams that filled the room halted.

I was left alone with Lena and she really was like a robot now. I had to try to get her back. I didn't know what to do. I could not touch her but I would just try to break through her.

"Lena." I whispered. Her head stared forward. "Lena, please look at me if you can." She turned curiously, and my heart leapt out of my chest, but then she turned back forward as if someone called for her to turn.

I continued to speak. "I need you to help me. Please. I don't know what else to do. I need you. You need me. I love you." She stared blankly so I tried once more. "We can get out of here. I can figure out how to make this stop. I promise you can be better and come back to me." Her eyes began to waver. I saw her hazel eyes for a split second before they glowed once more. I groaned in frustration.

Her eyes began flickering repeatedly until their glow shined through. What worked to bring her back last time? Even though this was a different control, I refused to believe that I couldn't bring Lena back myself.

Then I had an idea. She remembered my name when I triggered memories of me being mean to her. So I tried it because if it didn't work, there was no harm, no foul. "Lena. You were always so weak; so useless. I sent you here for a reason. I can't stand you." They were all lies, but I had to save her from this control. "Lena. You were a mistake. Your own father didn't want you to have anything to do with his plans."

She turned furiously at me, and I smirked because she was breaking through, but she had other ideas in mind. Her eyes bore into mine and I felt the pain that she was cursing upon me. It burned through me and I felt as if my insides were on fire. I moved my head as much as it would back and forth to make her lose her focus. It worked because it distracted her. Instead of boring her eyes into mine, she bore her eyes into the metal on accident.

To my surprised and to my advantage, a small piece fell to the ground, smoking and smoldering on the floor. I had to keep making her mad because she could find a way to get me out of this personal death trap.

"Don't you see how stupid you are?" I laughed as cruelly as I could manage. She continued to move her eyes down my body. A crack formed in the metal as she melted it with her eyes. I felt it loosen up but I didn't hear the delicate crack of it breaking off of me.

I was about to speak once more but just then, the doorknob started to turn. The door opened to reveal my father standing there. I was thankful that I couldn't hear Holland's cries any longer. Lena moved back into her position and continued her blank stare. And I acted as normal as I possibly could, while being trapped in metal and attempting an escape. I looked down to the metal that was cracked but he didn't seem to notice it was there.

"Good, you're still here." He smiled viciously. My throat constricted but I looked forward unfazed. "We have a visitor for you."

## Chapter Eighteen: Unexpected Visitor

GABE TORE INTO the room, fumbling to smack his self into the wall, after being shoved by Aiden. "Found him wandering around. He was trying to break into the building." Aiden said evenly.

Gabe smirked, his most famous look. "I would have if that idiot with green hair hadn't tried to help. He was an idiot. I swear I don't need help from anyone anyways." He smoothed his hair down and Aiden gripped both arms. He froze as his eyes found Lena. He smiled brightly at her and anger sprung up through me. "Jesus Christ. Jared, she is beautiful." I couldn't explain my anger. "Why did you have to get captured?" he asked me in an arbitrating way.

"Shut up." Dr. Ravana hit him over the head and Gabe looked mildly annoyed as he was chained up beside me. He didn't have blood pouring out of him, and I was grateful to not see him go through the same pain I did. Nothing went around his head either. I was sure he'd be surrounded in metal soon like I was.

"That's okay. We have someone else to get you." Gabe spat to Aiden.

182

I looked down. "No we don't." I told him simply.

Gabe looked over shocked. "Excuse me?" he said calmly but I could see that he was angry with me for revealing something so big.

"Holland has been captured. She was with me." Gabe's features changed through many emotions in that moment. He looked outraged and his mouth dropped open. I thought he was going to cry from how red his face became.

"What are you talking about?" Holland is at the safe house making weapons. This can't be. She was there before I left. She was there." He screamed now. His panicked stare searched the room, meeting the eyes of Aiden and then Dr. Ravana.

"Holland was with me this whole time. She tricked Kaley and we escaped the house that held Lena. She has been with me ever since. What's your deal? I am upset because all hope is gone now." I shook my head. "Holland is like a sister to me. She was captured and it's a fact, Gabe."

Gabe shook furiously. His whole body was jittering as if he just stepped out into the cold without a jacket. His teeth seemed to chatter in the exact same way and his eyes seemed to glaze over. "You lied to me!" I jumped in place from the severity in his voice. I thought he was speaking to me but he was looking right at my father. "You are all dead; do you hear me? Every last one of you! You lied to me!" He screamed scarier than I had ever heard him scream before. Come to think of it, he never screamed before this moment.

"Lied to you how?" I asked confused. "What are you talking about?" I cried out.

"They said we were the only ones captured. So I let them take me so Holland would save us. Damn it!" His eyes flickered to my face but somehow I didn't believe him. His cool demeanor had fallen. He loved Holland and that much I knew was true.

"Well. If that was your last hope then we're dead. Find a way to get us out." I said as quietly as I could.

Dr. Ravana cleared his throat. "Sorry to break the lover's quarrel. But we have to get to business." He didn't face us but I could tell by his voice that he was enjoying this. He wanted to see me break his whole life and he was probably going to get it.

He kept his back turned to us but spoke into the air. "Joseph will be back soon and let this be a fair warning." He paused. "If it isn't perfect, someone will suffer." He moved across the room to a large chair and sat. He put his hands behind his head. He watched us intently now. He looked at Gabe in a knowing way. "No one will break out of here when Lena is fully controlled. That includes both of you."

Aiden stepped over to Dr. Ravana. And looked at me with malevolent eyes. "Look, Jared, we can kill you now. Or let things get worse." He faced my dad with a laugh attempting to break through. "Although, it may be more fun to see you lose everything. What do you think dad?"

"I'd like to see him lose everything." They laughed in unison, and I cringed at it. I felt my anger bubbling up in my chest.

"Lena is still in there fighting." I spat at them. Aiden didn't budge but Dr. Ravana's face turned quickly to the book in his hands.

"We know that." Aiden said pleased. "That is why we created something new. She will never be able to speak again. Or think again. Or remember your face."

"I don't believe a word of it." I wanted to believe that I didn't but I did.

"Believe it. We had a genius create it." I looked over to Lena who cringed inwardly. I noticed it and felt chills on my arms. She was somehow still there. She was listening too. Although she still stared blankly, her body was able to move in a way that she couldn't if she were under full mind control. She knew who this genius was. I had to find out too.

Aiden fumed at the sight of this, and he bit down hard on his lip in concentration. He hit my father's arm slightly and pointed but my father had missed it already. Aiden dismissed it but stared down Lena as a result.

"I will fight to bring her back. Hope isn't lost completely." I said simply.

Aiden's eyes never left Lena's face as he approached me. He was near me but not close enough to touch me. "Lose hope, brother. Lose everything. Then we will kill you." I wished I could hit him but I thought of the only thing

I could do. I spat in his face as he had before. Gabe was chocking beside me as he stifled a laugh.

His face turned red before he turned to walk away. I smiled jubilantly but it quickly faded as he reached the desk. Aiden took the glass vase off the table behind him. My laugh was small and short. "Can't even punch me Aiden? You have to use a weapon so you don't ruin your hand." I mocked him but he already had his hand above his head, ready to strike me. He rushed to me. He mimicked my earlier smile as he finally let his hand slam down into my face. Glass busted all around me and I heard it crash to the ground.

He held the broken piece to my neck and I gasped as I felt it dig in a little. "Funny now?" he said and I opened my eyes to see red filled my vision. My unwillingness to answer seemed to be enough to make him angry again and he raised his hand once more, throwing the glass from my throat to the ground and lunging into to punch me in the nose. Blood gushed out, and I felt the blood trickling down my face. The warm blood entered my mouth and I squinted up to see him backing away. This certainly didn't seem like the last time I would be hit today.

*Prospect*

# Chapter Nineteen: Sacrifices

MY EYES WERE still fuzzy. I peered up only to see a black blurriness in my vision. The blackness blocking my view I knew was blood, but I could see enough. I focused slowly on the room in front of me. Aiden and my father were no longer in the room and I felt the heat flow to my face with embarrassment. Aiden had punched me and I couldn't do anything about it.

I felt stickiness on my ear, and figured it was more blood. I looked over to see Lena still beside me. I wished she was still reacting in some way, but she was now sitting on the ground, cross-legged. She looked bored. I looked to my left and saw that Gabe wasn't there in the room with me anymore, either. The shackles that helped hold him up where strewn across the floor with bright red fresh blood on them. Taking in my surroundings, I found red blotches all around the room. By the door, was a pool of blood, and I felt my stomach muscles clench up in alarm. What did they do to Gabe?

"Hey." I shouted loudly at Lena. She didn't even budge. I looked at her dazed face and felt frustration. "Hey." I screamed even louder. The door opened abruptly. Aiden walked in and jumped slightly with a startled look on his face. He looked angry when he heard my scream.

"What the hell are you screaming for? We should have glued your damn mouth shut again." He said with annoyance coloring his tone. He was carrying clothes.

"Again? If it actually worked then maybe you wouldn't have to repeatedly glue someone's mouth shut." He scowled. I was walking a thin line but I loved to pick at his scab. "Where is Gabe?" I asked, when he ignored my comment. He shrank back a little before stepping forward to face me. As he did so, a cackle escaped him. He looked fiercely down to Lena and her head turned on his command.

"Lena, would you like to do the honors?" When she didn't reply, he frowned. "I forgot." He cackled loudly. "You can't do anything on your own." He smiled to her as she turned her face back to the front.

"Well, Gabe wouldn't shut up so we shut him up." he said and I felt my eyes widen.

"Is he okay?" I asked weakly. I was overcome by my fatigue in that moment. My arms were completely asleep from being held up for so long and although Lena had loosened my suit of metal I was surrounded in, I was still uncomfortable.

"Jared. Why don't you just find out yourself?" He made a sarcastic look and put a finger to his mouth as if he were thinking. "Oh that's right. You can't find out."

I could feel bitter blood enter my mouth, and it tasted like the metals from before. "Let me out of here. You have me trapped because you know I could kill you all. And that makes you all a coward. You are all going to die once I get out of here. It's a fact."

"Oh yeah? Then why didn't you grace us with your scary methods to kill us before we trapped you? Is it because you are incapable of any physical action that would mortally damage any of us?" He lunged forward towards me. I didn't even jump. He was acting stronger because I was trapped. "You can't win Jared. Do us all a favor and stop trying. Now." he said darkly.

"I wanted to see if she was okay. If she was alive before I killed you." I spat back at him, it wasn't a lie, but I didn't kill them because I didn't know enough. If they were dead, how would I even stop the disease or their control over others? "I won't give up and you will be dead." I tried my best to look as callous as I could but I didn't have the capability to be as evil as he was.

Aiden looked to Lena while placing a hand on the side of her face. He began caressing her face as he did before and she stared unchanging forward. For some reason I could have sworn that she tensed up at his touch. Then he did something unthinkable. I began thrashing in my suit. He began to lift her shirt off, my shirt. Exposing her bra. He quickly slipped on her new tank top and helped her in a cardigan. My heart was pounding my chest. "Get your fucking hands off her." I said through gritted teeth.

He smiled deeply into her eyes. Her unseeing eyes. I grinded my teeth. I wished Lena had burnt my suit more to get me the hell out of there.

"Well, you don't have to worry about her dying. She is a necessity." He ignored me. I still struggled to move my body. Any part of my body out of the suit. He looked at her with admiring eyes and I felt my heart pounding. I hoped she didn't admire him back when she had forgotten about me. "You, on the other hand, are a pain in the ass." He paused and met my eyes. I willed myself to keep staring at them. The truth was, they were nothing like my eyes. His were black. They looked evil. I had to admit it. I didn't remember them ever looking so blacked out. I thought we had the same eyes. I looked at the shape of his face, exactly like mine.

I couldn't believe we were so similar and I hated to say that he was my brother through and through. "I don't think anyone would miss you. Maybe I could kill you now instead of dad doing it." He didn't drop his hand from her face and I wanted to slap it away but I was still trapped here. I knew I would die and I knew most of all that I had failed. I didn't find any answers and let Lena suffer in consequence to this.

After what seemed like an eternity, he let his hand drop. I sensed my heart rate slowing along with my breath, and felt my shoulders slump. He walked in long strides away from me. When he reached the desk, he quickly turned to me. When he locked eyes with me once more, he was holding a knife.

Fear spread through me. Before I could even think of what to do, he was running towards me. I don't mean just running, I mean a wild man with his arms outstretched in the air was running towards me. The knife was raised above his hand and was held as if he were about to go to battle in a war.

All I could think was that I would not die a coward. I would not scream. I would feel the pain and I would not scream. I would not give him the satisfaction of knowing I was afraid of my death. As he approached me, I didn't cringe away, and I felt that this would decrease his satisfaction.

He was level with my left eye. His face smirked up as the knife abruptly stopped inches away from my face. I was blinking frantically at the knife before my face. The knife was just about to pierce my eye but that was when laughter erupted from him as he backed away. He was a lunatic in the most rare form. Had he always been that way, or had my father driven him mad?

"I always wanted to see who would kill you and how. I have thought of killing you for a long time." Aiden said as he twisted the knife between his hands. He let the point press into his forefinger, and I watched him make a tiny pierce on his hand. Blood was about to spill but that was when he neared the knife again towards my right eye this time before letting it falter.

"Why do you hate me Aiden?" I said to him. The knife was down to his side and I felt myself take a deep breath of relief.

For a moment, I thought I sensed some type of apprehension. I watched as he turned into thirty different people before finally resorting back to anger. He shoved the knife to my throat.

"You lied to me. You always were the favorite. You had everyone's love. You were mom's favorite. I wouldn't die without being someone's important person. I have a purpose now. I will die being important, where as you will die for love and a pitiful love at that." He forced his glare over to Lena. " And what a worthless love it is. She is worthless and I am going to be extraordinary. People will shout my name. The glory is all mine, Jared. Not yours and your tramp. No one will remember you or her. Most of all, they won't remember your love."

"Aiden, rethink this. Walk away now. People will shout your name because they have to and not because they want to." He moved the knife closer to me and I felt the coldness of the blade, but I continued to speak. "I found love and something worth having and dying for. You are controlling people and ruining people's lives. I have saved a life and made mine worth living." His face fell as well as the knife, but he retreated back to normal and quickly he raised the knife again.

"I don't care what you say Jared. I will make one of them love me if I get lonely." He told me quietly. I felt sorry for him in that moment. He was still a monster though.

"Aiden, that isn't real love, like what Lena and I have." He shook his head furiously in disagreement but I continued anyways. "Yes, still have. I know she feels it inside her still."

"Ah, then maybe I will make Lena love me. Since she had such a great love, she could probably portray that love to me. She won't remember you anyways when you're dead. She won't remember you at all after this new enhancement, then she can be mine." He laughed and turned the knife up to my throat. I felt the tip digging into my throat. "Say goodbye Jared. They say you can see all your loved ones when you die. Tell mom hi for me." He snorted and I felt my breath take as he pushed harder into my throat. "Or don't."

This was it. This was my last second of breath. That was when he moved up my face towards my eyes again. He was going to stab my eye out. I looked straightforward. I would not die a coward. I would die brave like Lena would. I sent her here and now she was being punished because of me. This was my entire fault. I let everyone down. Dr. Alona would look down ashamed at me if he could.

It was in a blink of an eye. There was a knife in front of me, forcing its way up my face and me completely defenseless. Before I knew it, there was a hand holding Aiden's hand where the knife was. I heard the crack before I could register that Aiden's wrist was just broken. The white of his bone was poking through his skin. I had the urge to vomit in that moment.

That was when I saw her; Lena stepped in front of me. Her beauty was still enticing to me and she was so smooth in her attacks; so brave and cunning, new qualities that suited her well. Her eyes were glowing and Aiden dropped the knife from his damaged hand, holding it with wide eyes. He screamed as he fell to the floor. *He acts so dramatic.* Lena turned on him. Aiden was thrashing around on the floor. Lena was using her powers on him, burning him as she did to me earlier. There was something intense in this power. As soon as she stared at you, your insides were practically on fire.

"Don't ever touch him again." She spoke with a magical voice. Each syllable came out as if she were a snake. She held his hair in her hands and jerked up, all while ripping some of his hair from his precious head. "Understand?" She asked. Before he had a millisecond to answer, she slapped his head down to the ground with a loud thud. Blood spilled from his nose. "That's for hitting him when he couldn't fight back, you piece of shit."

He writhed on the ground, and she let out a laugh. Almost as cruel as his was once before. Her anger wasn't over because as soon as she stood, she lifted her foot in a smooth action while kicking the side of him. It was so hard that he fell over to the side, smacking his head once more to the ground. She was too strong for her own good, but at this point it worked to her advantage.

"And this is for touching me." She kicked him right in between the legs. That was when tears fell down his face. I could tell he was blacking out, and I couldn't help but laugh.

She turned her face to me when she heard me and I saw her in there. She was no longer Lena, the brainwashed girl but instead she was my Lena. Her eyes seemed to dim a little but I felt my mouth actually drop. Her eyes glowed, but instead of being emerald, they glowed her hazel eyes. The same hazel eyes I fell in love with.

## Chapter Twenty: Consider This A Sign

SHE WAS WORKING faster than I thought a human could ever work, but she wasn't human, not anymore. "We have to escape right now." She told me frantically as she pulled on each chain but I was in a daze. She groaned in frustration as she gazed hard at the metal suit I was in and I felt a prick of heat but I was still lost. I wasn't moving and I saw her pull hard on the chains around my wrists. I felt them release my wrists and looked down to see small bloody holes in my wrists.

Before I knew it, I was dropped from the suit and she ripped the cardigan from her body. She tore it in half and wrapped my wrists to keep the blood in. Although, I was sure I was no longer bleeding. I was going to tell her this but before I knew it she ran into my arms. I felt her tug my hair and I looked down to her. She stared in my eyes and I felt the disbelief spreading through me. I pulled her lips to mine.

"I love you. You're back." I said against her lips. My voice was a whisper but she looked at me with indulgent eyes.

"I love you, too." She held my gaze but she quickly went back to grimacing again. She was scared, but she tried

197

hard not to show it. "Come on." She jolted Aiden once more for good measure and he groaned again. It looked like he was slowly losing consciousness.

We ran quickly towards the desk at the back of the room. There was a window behind it, Lena had continued to stare out of it the whole time, and I wasn't surprised to only see the ocean from it. She put her hand up towards the window and to my surprise the window burst open. She looked down at her hand in amazement as her necklace started to move a little. She stepped up with ease onto the ledge and reached for my hand as I glided up beside her.

I looked ahead and could not see any sign of land. She started shaking and I gripped her hand, "What's the matter?" I asked cautiously but before she answered I saw a red glow that seemed to light up her features. There was red all around her face as the ocean sprayed up. "Water." she stopped her shaking as the water splashed up. We were up many stories, but the water seemed to spray up high, even though we were on an island.

"It hurts. I can't go across it. I normally can but." She stopped short. She moved her hand above the water and it glowed a red. She gasped and moved her hand back in, clutching it to her chest before showing me the red welts rising on her hand. "We're stuck here." She said calmly before closing her eyes tightly while shaking her head. "No, I am stuck here." She reopened them and looked at me longingly. "Leave while you can. Please. Leave me right now." She reached her hand towards me and I felt them touch my chest. "Save yourself. Get me out of here when you're more prepared. I can wait. I will wait."

I looked behind me. They would know we escaped soon. "No." I said calmly but I felt scared. "I am not leaving you here to die. They will kill you. You don't have the answers they need. That's what they think at least."

She shook her head and I reached her face to comfort her. Her skin was alarmingly cold but I felt warmth in my body from just touching her. The water was cold and she was as well, in that moment I wanted to feel for her pulse. I wanted to know if she still had a heartbeat. I knew for a fact that she still had love for me so I knew somewhere inside her was a beating heart; even if it only beat slowly, even if it weren't a necessity for her to live. I knew it was there. I knew she couldn't cry anymore but even still, her lip began to quiver. "Jared, please. I am not going to let you die. You have to escape. You have to leave right now."

I wasn't going anywhere and she knew it. She began shaking her head when I didn't respond. She bit down on her lip about to speak but I held up my hand. "Wait." I said curiously. "How did you get across the water when you were under control?" I asked.

"I have no idea. I mean every time I passed through, I wasn't always told what to do. But my eyes would go black. I was sort of blinded." She shook her head as if deep in thought.

"Lena. You have to be controlled to be able to move. You're trapped here if you aren't controlled." I said to her with angst in my voice.

Her face turned up in frustration. "I can't leave then. If Dr. Ravana won't activate it then I am stuck here." She looked miserably at me. "I won't be able to. You said it yourself; I have to be controlled to leave this place. Please leave. Live your life." She shrugged her shoulders and looked away from me quickly.

I frowned and lifted my hands to her face. I cupped her chin in them and forced her to look at me. "There is not a life without you. You stay; I stay. My life is here beside you. Figuring out how to help you." She frowned deeply as her brow furrowed. "Plus there really isn't much a life to live, with all the robots and mind control. Not to mention rotting skin disease." She rolled her eyes and I held in a laugh. *That's just like her.*

"I don't know how long I have control over myself." She said calmly. "What if I just turn on you? It is dangerous for me to leave at all." She looked over her shoulders in a nervous way. "Why haven't they checked on us in a while?"

I shrugged my shoulders about to respond. I felt a gust of wind pushing us both forward to the edge of the ledge. Lena glowed bright red, and I reached for the sides of the building as I cowered down to cover my eyes from her brightness. She seemed to be tumbling forward, about to fall to the water. I watched as her skin began to blister from the mist of the ocean.

She screamed in pain, and I looked on in shock. Finally, I came to my senses and I reached for her to pull her back to safety but as soon as her hand touched mine, I felt the heat burning through me. My hands seemed to blister just as hers were doing. I was being burned in the process of trying to save her. I grunted loudly but kept a firm grip. I felt my hand scalding and was alarmed to see skin beginning to flake off. "Grab my other hand!" I screamed to her.

"No. I am burning you." She yelled to me as she attempted to let go of my other hand. I only gripped her tighter. "Let me go!" She screamed over the loud waves beating against the building now. The water was coming up on the island and I stared in disbelief. It seemed as if a storm was brewing.

"I don't care. Reach for me." I shouted through gritted teeth. She shook her head furiously until I grabbed a hold of her and jerked her. I screamed as pain burned through my hands. It felt like I was on fire but I wouldn't let her fall to her death either. I yelped in pain as she touched my arm as she finally regained her balance.

"I can't feel my arm anymore." She said lightly before facing me. "How are your hands though?" she reached for them but stopped herself quickly. "I am so sorry. I will heal fast, but you won't." She shook vigorously. I looked to her hands to see that there were dull scabs on them.

"What was that wind? Jared, what is our plan? I have no clue what to do? Will we have to fight them? I can take them now." It finally clicked with me that she wasn't someone who needed protecting anymore. "We're wasting time." She shouted to me when I did not answer.

"Okay first off, we are going to have to escape on something that won't let the water touch your body but it will be painful for you. What do you say? We can find something." She smiled weakly to me but then panic filled her features. She backed away from me.

"What?" I asked but she put a hand up to silence me.

A whooshing sound took over as I was silenced again. "Hush." I remained quiet and listened to a sound that only sounded like wind to me. "Where did it come from?" she asked puzzled and I laughed.

"There is a storm coming. Don't be paranoid." I said and she held up a hand to cease my laughter.

"Quick, where do we need to get to? We can climb the ledge to it." She faced me head on and pierced me with her hazel eyes. "Where do we need to be Jared?" She asked impatiently.

"We have to get on that bridge to leave. The one Gabe was on. He said something about a bridge. Where is it? If he was on it then it has to be important." I said to her.

"Simple enough. That is a piece of cake. It is just around the building. Stay close to me and we can make it. I'll burn a little but who cares? We can escape." She said excited and my heart warmed at the thought. Only for a second because we weren't free yet but we would be as free as we could be at this point.

"Let's go." I smiled and leaned in as I kissed her cheek. As we started to make our ascent around the building, an unseen force lurched us against the wall. We were trapped tight on the ledge. All of the sudden, as though we were puppets on lassos, we were being pulled towards the window. They had found us. We had taken too much time to make our move.

We froze as we entered the room again. There wasn't just Dr. Ravana waiting for us but an entire army. Lena gasped and clasped her hand over her mouth. Some unknown force tied us up together. We didn't care who it was that touched us and kicked us around because what we saw made us both fall flat on our ass.

# Chapter Twenty-One: Cruel World

I COULDN'T BELIEVE what I was seeing. Lena just looked startled but most of all she looked angry. She grabbed my hand and squeezed. Her grip on me was so tight that I flinched away slightly. I didn't know if I would have any feeling left in it when her grip would loosen. I didn't care too much because what stood before me was the most frightening thing I had ever seen.

I looked ahead into his eyes and couldn't believe what I saw. His eyes were bloodshot red as if he had popped every last blood vessel in his eyes. The strange thing was, his pupils were the color of red as well. "Gabe? Is that you? You look awful." I said questionably.

I whispered slowly to Lena. I was afraid to make any sudden movements because they would probably attack us. "They've got Gabe now." I said to her and she shook her head all while looking completely unsurprised. She stared to him unchanging and with little sympathy, which I didn't understand.

She didn't turn to me but she spoke quietly. "No they didn't." Gabe twisted into a sickening smile. His teeth were brighter than normal. They shined whiter and were completely straight. Lena let go of my hand in the slightest bit. I think she let go from the shock of how repulsive he looked.

"Well, Jared." Gabe spoke in an angelic tone like Lena's voice had changed to when her eyes tended to glow. "Lena knows all about this. I paid her a few visits when she was under control. She didn't tell you?" he smiled, and it was malicious. It was not Gabe. It couldn't be him really.

"What are you talking about?" I asked in shock. Lena froze beside me, I could feel her shaking and I couldn't tell if it were tears that couldn't be spilt building up or wrath beyond her control.

"We need to leave now." She said through her tight lip line. "Burns and all." Before I knew it she was lunching us both into the air. Even though we were tied together, she still somehow got us off the ground. She flew towards the window but when we both stepped foot onto the ledge, still tied together, we were jerked back again just like before.

The force was so strong; it jerked my head back too fast, making me extremely dizzy. I lost my balance and fell to the ground hard, hitting my chin on a piece of glass. I had no idea where it came from until I looked to Lena who had shards of glass all over her. She had busted through the window during her flight to get me out of there and I hadn't even noticed.

I got up quickly to see that I had glass sticking out of my arm. I felt my vision waver as I stood up. I felt jolted for a second before regaining some of my glassy vision back.

Holding myself up was a challenge. I was about to reach down to help Lena, but then I saw that Lena was no longer beside me.

That was when she began to scream. Not just any scream, an earth shattering scream. Every single person in the room fell backwards. She tugged my hand, and I was lurched into the air. But then I was being pulled back. Joseph had me in a headlock.

Lena stayed floating in the air. "Go without me." I shouted to her. But she didn't. She dropped instantly to the ground and then Gabe jerked Lena to his body. She didn't even fight it.

Gabe had his arm around Lena's neck, holding Lena in place as he sneered at me. I was taken aback by how angry he looked. "Ah good, you're watching." Before I had time to even take a breath, he took Lena's neck between his hands and twisted. The twist was so powerful that it was all it took. The delicate crunch made me know that it was too late to help her.

It was as if time stood still as Lena fell lifelessly to the ground. She slammed on the ground with a loud thud. I could not move because I didn't want to believe it was real. I fell to the floor uselessly. Joseph let me go with ease. I crawled to her. I felt my heart breaking with each crawl. When I reached her, I covered my mouth. I reached down and held her head up and knew that she was gone.

She was really gone. Her eyes were wide open. They were hazel, which comforted me in a way. She died herself;

they weren't fluttering as they were before and they never would again. Her head was lying limp in my heads. I didn't feel sad. I felt rage. "Now, do you see the difference between me and my friends?" he spoke again.

"They did this to you." I said through my teeth. "You killed her. You really just killed her." I couldn't bare the words. I couldn't face the fact that I would be without her. I stared down at her in shock.

"Did this to me?" he laughed cruelly and without feeling. "Oh, Jared, come on. Would I really ever be captured?" I looked up quickly to meet his bloodcurdling eyes. "Ah, agreeing with me." he smirked and I felt a scowl come on my face. He continued without a moment's hesitation. "Did this to me? No, I did this to myself."

"Yourself? Why would you do this to yourself? I have known you my whole life. You would never do this." I turned to my father and his crowd who were all looking pretty satisfied. "Stop making him lie to me." I shouted to my father, but he only watched on. He turned his head as if he were a curious dog hearing a strange noise. He did not say a word to me.

"You are so naïve. Your dad, with no special characteristics other than being a surgeon, could create and mediate a robotic arm?" I felt the truth registering in my brain.

He continued on. "Your dad, with no special skills could find a way to control centrally every human being on the planet. Jared, please. We both know that there is only one person in this room who could do all of these things. Do you really think your dad could come up with this? Get the codes to get into Lena's pathetic dad's computer?" He turned to Dr. Ravana and I looked on with disgust. "No offense."

Lena's head suddenly weighed fifty more pounds. I froze. I don't think I even took a breath. I sat Lena's head down gently on the ground, leaving a last kiss upon her cheek. I got to my feet slowly. Gabe followed my eyes all the way up. I looked between my father and Gabe as they looked pleased with one another as they nodded heads. "You guys act like you're such good friends, but did you forget that he turned you into one of them so he could control you." I said challengingly.

"You still don't get it, do you?" Gabe said after a long silence. "I control them now. I control all of them." He laughed menacingly. He stepped a little closer to me, but not close enough for me to reach him. "Look in my eyes. I am the main controller now." I looked into his red eyes. They were shockingly demon like. It seemed that my friend, Gabe, was no longer in there. Or maybe he was this way all along?

"Why would he give you that power?" I asked reproachfully.

"I created the robotic arm." He screeched loudly before focusing again. He looked like a manic and a man who was losing his mind. "I am the creator of this "cure." Her father created the disease, your father spread it around and I created the cure to control everyone. Come on now.

Get smart. You are so pathetic. Just like her father." He nodded towards Lena on the ground.

He circled me and kicked Lena to the side as he approached me. She slammed against the wall. Nothing was between Gabe and I now. I wanted to kill him, in the most painful way. "I let him have his fun but this was my show from the very beginning." He menacingly moved closer to my face. "Aren't you afraid now? I can snap you in two like Lena."

I didn't move away from him. "Why did you do this? We were friends." I said simply, trying hard to keep my hurt under control. It was all I could say. He was my friend.

"No hard feelings, but I want to be the ruler of the world and I will be with this. I will destroy everything and rule all that remains." He looked down at Lena against the wall. "But enough of this, Lena is of vital importance and she is under my control now."

I blinked twice in confusion. "Lena is dead. You just killed her." Somehow I felt a strike of hope. Even if Lena was controlled, it meant she was alive.

"Ha. Not quite." He said simply and lifted his hand up as if he were commanding a symphony. "Rise." Lena swiftly picked up her head as if she were just in a mere sleep this whole time. She looked up to me and I gasped. Her eyes glowed red just as Gabe's did. She sneered an evil smile to me and joined her master's side.

## Chapter Twenty-Two: Never Enough

I WILLED MYSELF to believe that my eyes were deceiving me. I couldn't decide if I were thrilled to see her alive or disgusted to see that she would never be the same.

"To be controlled by me, they have to merely die." Gabe smiled to me menacingly. "It's simple really. They don't even have to die by my hands. As long as they have "the cure," they are sent to my control. Their bodies had to be completely vulnerable. So, Lena is under my control now. Forever."

He spoke the last word and I felt shivers running through my body as he faced me. His inflamed eyes were shinning at me and I didn't look away even though I wanted to.

My father stepped forward and for the first time, he wasn't the person I hated the most. He placed his hand on Gabe's shoulder as he whispered into his ear. I looked away to catch another look at Lena.

She was staring at me but this time there was no longing or confusion in her eyes. She glared me down, and I felt sick as I realized she might hate me as much as everyone else in the room. The whites of her eyes were nonexistent and they seemed to have blood in them. Gabe spoke up, and I jumped from the bitterness in his voice. "Dr. Ravana and I have your life to discuss. Don't mind us."

"Should we keep him alive? To make sure she really is fully controlled?" Gabe said as quietly as he could. If Gabe was evil, what did that mean about Holland? Did she know or was she in on this? I shivered at the thought.

I didn't listen to their hushed voices any longer because I didn't really care about my fate. I knew I had to find a way out to get Lena out of this. She had to be in there still. She'd gotten out from their control before and she could do it again. I had to believe that.

I searched the faces of the new members around Gabe. Their eyes were still emerald green. I noticed with a pit of sadness in my stomach that Lena's eyes were the only ones glowing a bright red. I looked into each of their faces and jumped a little when I saw one staring at me directly. All the other members' faces were erected to the front except for him. I turned my head curiously while frowning deeply.

He had green hair. I remembered him from earlier, and he now looked questionably at me, turning his head to mimic me. He nodded his head slightly to show me that he was aware and awake. I looked at him and he turned his head to the side, nodding towards Gabe.

I had to speak to him. He continued to nod towards Gabe, and I was about to mouth to him *"what?"* But before I knew it, he was lunging for Gabe.

Gabe tumbled to the ground and the green haired boy nailed Gabe in the nose. There was no blood spilt from Gabe, and his eyes fumed. His nose was broken, it lurched over to the side but he did not bleed. It didn't seem to faze him. The only reaction from Gabe was a grunt of frustration before he slammed his hand into the boy's nose. The green haired boy did not give up because he reached around and locked Gabe in a chokehold before smashing his head into the wall beside them.

I was ready to grab Lena and whisk us away but she suddenly reacted as Gabe's head hit the wall. She reached out with a speed that was completely otherworldly and slammed the boy into the same wall that Gabe had just picked himself up from. Gabe regained his composure as he straightened out his collar. I watched as he took his hands and cracked his nose back into place. He let out a strangled cough as he recovered his breath.

Meanwhile, the boy was struggling to break free from Lena's death grip around his shirt. Lena picked him off the ground as soon as she saw that he had his fist ready to punch her, but he dropped it and tried to pry her off of him. "Lena, please." He struggled to speak. "Remember yourself. I know I thought we were angels but we are weapons. We are not protectors; look at all we have destroyed. They are ruining us. Don't be like them." He cried to her. She reached for his neck to shut him up. I was startled by his words. She jerked him away from her quickly as if a command were spoken. I was sure there was.

She released his neck. Red handprints remained on his neck where she had held him. He held his hand to his throat and let out jagged breaths. I caught sight of Gabe looking intently to the scene before him, and realized he was not even breaking contact from them. No doubt, controlling the entire situation.

I watched Lena's eyes the entire time and saw that the color never faded. She was lost. Lena grabbed the boy once more around the neck and the boy went limp in her arms. Dr. Ravana seemed to have had enough because he jerked the green haired boy away from her, tossing him on the ground behind him. He snapped a finger to Lena and pointed down at the boy. I watched as Lena picked him up from the ground and she dragged him from the room unconscious.

Gabe turned to Dr. Ravana. His eyes were wide. "Where are they taking him?" his eyes faltered for a second, as if he were trying to find his feelings again but I knew he couldn't find them because of all the pain he caused without another thought.

"Oh, where everyone who disobeys goes." He dismissed him with a look. "You'll see that room soon." My father waved his hand to Gabe to tell him to not worry about it. Gabe nodded and took a deep breath. His chest rose and fell before he faced forwards, his eyes boring into mine.

"Now," Dr. Ravana demanded, it came out as a whisper around the room, "tell Lena to keep Jared under control." Gabe obeyed because in a blink of an eye, Lena was at my side again at once. She jerked my arm and I tumbled to the ground. She lay right on top of me, pinning me to the ground. I felt the coldness on the floor and looked up to Gabe, only to have my face slapped down to the floor by Lena. She was so strong that I could not move even if I wanted to. I had imagined Lena so close to me but in a much different way.

"Well, that is just too easy." Dr. Ravana spoke with humor in his tone as he glided past me, kicking my nose a little when he passed. My nose was broken from Aiden. I knew it had to be. All I could move was my eyes and the blood built on the floor. Maybe I would get lucky and die from too much loss of blood.

"I need to see Holland." I said loudly with little feeling into the floor. I had to know if she were in on this too. Gabe glanced up with wide eyes. With the creepy red eyes, he looked scarier than anything else.

"Holland?" he asked with a tad bit of panic coloring his voice. He regained composure by even brushing back his hair. "Holland was escorted out of the building to safety." Gabe said. Dr. Ravana shushed him. I could feel the pressure building in the room.

"Wasn't she?" he said softly.

"I don't know! They took her away." I said loudly with annoyance, Lena finally let me look up. "Now, where is she? I want to be with her and make sure she is okay." Gabe turned slowly to Dr. Ravana, who was grinning widely.

"She was not a part of this. I thought I made that clear before we transferred networks." Gabe said angrily, I felt the hairs on my back standing up.

"Oh. Holland is a little preoccupied. If you'd like to see her, I will gladly get her in here." He said serenely and Gabe looked unfazed.

"I want to see her. Bring her here." I said as if he were speaking to me. Lena picked up my head lightly from the floor and slammed it down. I felt my lip busting open and licked my lip to feel the blood from it. I spat out the blood that was filling my mouth from the impact.

Dr. Ravana walked to his desk and picked up a phone. He spoke into his phone and as soon as his lips left the phone, the doors burst open. He put his phone back on the receiver and sat down in his chair. He lifted his feet up to the desk and crossed them with satisfaction.

Max walked in jerking a limping girl behind him. He finally put her in front of us and I gasped out loud. This couldn't be Holland because Holland never would look so out of order. Her hair was ratty and tangled in a mess. Her head hung low and it looked as if she were never going to be able to lift her head again.

She appeared weak because Max was the only thing holding her up at all, and she was crying. I had never seen her cry in my entire life. She looked up to me as the tears gathered into her eyes. I couldn't see her as clearly as I could without Lena holding my head down. From what I could see I knew something wasn't right. She had a hand covering her face and I thought it was to continue to wipe her eyes, but that wasn't it.

That was when I smelt it. The smell wasn't something you could forget. Lena reeked of it for days at the safe house, near the very end. It was a smell of blood mixed with the smell of decay of a body. Holland had Dermadecatis. I looked as much as I could. The bullet hole wound was black. She moved her hand away from her face, and I saw her whole cheek had started to rot. I put my head down and let out a whimper. I heard Holland sob louder as soon as my head faced the floor. I knew I was probably soaking myself in blood but I didn't care anymore. "I'm sorry." She shouted to me.

"Sorry for what?" I asked through gritted teeth. "This isn't your fault. Look to the precious one in front of you." I groaned with my lips completely on the ground.

"What are you talking about? The precious one?" I left my head down and realized she must not have seen Gabe's eyes yet.

"Gabe." I said to her. I lifted my head back up just to see her reaction. Her eyes widened.

"Gabe?" she asked in surprise.

"Yes. Me." Gabe said loudly, as he turned to face her. Astonishment registered on Holland's face. I watched as his demeanor changed through my restricted vision. He looked frightened, even with his red eyes. He looked frightened of Holland, who I believed he once loved. Not anymore.

## Chapter Twenty-Three: Go Where Our Problems Won't Follow

SHE DIDN'T SPEAK for a long time. Her head was hanging low as she stood with Max holding her. She was sobbing, and it was silently but I could see her shoulders shaking furiously.

"Why?" she screamed after a long time. "How could you do this? I trusted you. No, we trusted you." She looked to me and I shook my head and looked down to avoid the hurt in her eyes. I was betrayed but I knew Holland cared for Gabe in a different way. "You are an abomination. I hate you Gabe Mitchell. I hate you. How could you do this to us? I hope you die." She bawled. He cringed a little but Dr. Ravana moved from his lounged position to look at Gave straight on in disappointment. Gabe caught sight of Dr. Ravana's eyes and looked fiercely forward.

"Did you ever love me?" she asked weakly. I looked to him, hoping somewhere in his cold heart that he wouldn't hurt Holland more.

He didn't hesitate. "No." she buried her head back down and didn't lift up again. She was trembling from the tears and I could tell anger was building up in her because her breath became uneven as it did when she couldn't handle a situation.

I felt that it was my time to speak; if not for me, for Holland. "You know so much about us. We will die because you know us so well. But I want you to look back at what you're leaving behind." I said to him.

"I have left nothing important behind. I don't really care what I've left behind." He said and held my gaze long before he looked to Holland just a second too long for my liking. He opened the door and still looked at her. He left the room in the blink of an eye but Dr. Ravana stayed behind.

"Isn't it great how things can turn out?" His smile was nauseating. I didn't respond. I watched Holland. She finally turned to me, ignoring my father's presence all together.

"I really loved him. How stupid of me." She sniffed in before continuing. "I have been with him this whole time. I never left his side and he was with them the whole time. How could I have not been suspicious?"

"I don't understand what happened to make him do this."

Dr. Ravana answered for us and I clenched my teeth at his voice. "Oh, Gabe was a part of my internship in the summer, just as Joseph was. He was a genius at the age of nine. He was a little boy, Jared's age. He was far beyond the wits of teenagers and he said he wanted to be a scientist or a doctor. I told him he could be better than that. He was so smart. He believed in me. He was your friend by the chance of God." He smirked down to us. "Gabe wasn't your friend when he moved into the safe house. He was working for me the entire time. His friendship with you only made things easier for me."

"Why did he agree to be a traitor? What did you give him?" I asked.

"Pure protection and power you can only dream of." He said simply while shrugging his shoulders. "Well, until I see it is necessary to give it to him." He walked over and before I knew it, he jerked my head up by my hair. "But he is fooled, he doesn't see that I don't think of him as a son. I see him as a weapon that was used and that his time will be spent. It is only a matter of time." he turned to Holland. "What a shame, you could have been great. You would have been a beautiful addition to the family." He chuckled before letting go of my hair.

Holland spoke up. "I don't see how this is a family when you will dispose of those who are not important any longer."

"I don't care what you think. I care what I get in the end. They know that. I have told them from the beginning. And if they don't listen, I have a master mind beside me." He backed up.

"But I know him." She told him. "I know his hopes and dreams. He loved me, you know?" she said softly.

"Because I asked him to." Dr. Ravana told her. He backed away and Holland's face registered the truth of it all.

"I guess I will give you time to let your broken heart heal." He smiled to her and she shuttered beside me.

We were left on the floor, and Holland began laughing weakly. I looked amazed at her. She moved the slightest bit in Max's arms. I frowned at her. I couldn't have her going crazy on me. She laughed crazed again.

"What on earth could you be laughing at?" I said impatiently to her. I sighed in annoyance.

"How much do you want to save her?" Holland asked and locked eyes with me.

"I'll do anything." I said.

"Thought you'd say something like that." She shifted herself once more in Max's arms. "Then forgive me."

I felt myself panic but then she was moving her hand in the slightest bit. Before I knew it, I felt Lena's weight being lifted off of me and I shot up as fast I could in that moment. When I looked around, I couldn't find Lena. I searched around me until I looked to the ceiling. Lena was wrapped in rope, while being held in place to the ceiling. It must have been the same weapon that brought Lena and me back in earlier. Her mouth was tapped shut as well as Max beside her, who was wrapped as well.

"What was that?" I whispered through the silence.

"Gabe left me weapons. What an idiot." She laughed insanely as she jerked me forward with the pull of her hand. We reached the window's ledge that I was just at with Lena.

"We're flying. Let's go." She pulled from her side a tiny device. She turned it over once in her hand and clicked it on. It turned into a jet pack and she grabbed my arm hastily. The smoke built in the air as I saw figures run in the room behind us, shouting.

We flew into the air before I could see who it was, and I held onto Holland for dear life as the pack jolted forward. "Where is there to go?" I screamed over the noise.

"No clue. I have no idea where we are. We will just fly." I looked behind me to see many figures flying behind me. They all shouted in surreal voices, they told us to "come back" and "surrender."

We soared through the sky, and I felt safe for a second before being slammed in the back of the head. My vision blurred, and I felt myself losing grip on Holland before she shouted in my ear to wake me back up. There was a second blow and as I slung forward, I let go of Holland.

The fall was fast, and for a moment, I welcomed death. I looked up to see Holland as she dived down to catch me. She caught me under the armpits, and I was held in place. As I clutched onto Holland, I looked behind me to see fifteen creatures tailing us. They were the robots that Lena was now, some had red eyes and some had emerald eyes.

I was ready to attack them when I caught my eyes on a pair of bright red eyes. Then I felt the fire I was prepared for. However, I wasn't prepared for a more excruciating pain. It was as if someone was breaking every bone in my body while setting me on fire. When I finally found the strength to close my eyes, I had an idea.

"Holland. Fly towards the ocean now!" I shouted to her and still felt the pain.

She obeyed me, and I felt the mist of the ocean as we soared closer to it. I looked up to find that only one followed us as the others kept their distance from the water. I touched the water with my feet as the robot continued down. It was a boy and I didn't recognize his face. His eyes were red, and I wondered how many others had to die. Gabe was forming his own army of red-eyed freak soldiers. I kicked as much water on him as I could with my feet.

His face turned a bright red and steam escaped his ears. Blisters formed as soon as the steam stopped. He cried in pain and backed up as I continued to kick water up at him. He barely escaped the last splash of water and he flew to meet his crew above.

Holland and I stayed there for a while because none of the other robots soared down after seeing what happened. Holland looked menacingly up at them. "I hate them all." She said in a chilled voice.

I looked into the air to see that they were gone. We decided to keep moving for what seemed like an hour. We soared close to the water. We finally saw something in the distance. As we approached it, I felt myself sigh in relief.

"We need to land there." I told Holland.

"I don't think we can make it there. The jetpack is losing speed." Just as she said this, the jetpack made a pitiful sound. We caught each other's eyes. Then we dropped.

We hit the water hard. I went under the water to feel relief. When I rose back up, I heard screams of horror. My heart started beating fast, and out of my periphery, I caught sight of Holland panicking.

"What's wrong?" I shouted through the waves crashing down.

"Water burns." She said between screams. I knew there wasn't anything I could do to help except to help her swim to the island. As I grabbed her and attempted to lead her to the island, she pushed away from me. I reached frantically for her hand and heard her screams growing more intense.

She pulled something out of her pocket. It was neon yellow and a small circle. Through the screams we were elevated out of the water. I jolted in shock as I realized that we were in a raft. Gabe must have given her a lot of gadgets to use.

"I forgot about this one." She said through gasps.

We floated a little. The waves were too much, and we needed to reach the land. I was going to tell Holland this but she had other plans. Holland laid her back on the raft. Some water splashed up, and I got in front of her to avoid it hitting her square on again.

"I can't do this. I feel like Lena. I feel weak and I won't let them control me." She said softly to me. I didn't answer. Instead I sat down on the float.

She continued. "We have to stop them. You know we can. We don't need Gabe. We just need each other." She climbed closer to me. "We can do this." She looked me right in the eyes and nodded. I was taken aback.

As if she read my mind, she continued. "I know you're unsure and don't think you can do this, but you're a genius too. You were in charge before you left and brought Lena back. You built the machines Gabe wanted created. We don't need him." She spoke softly to me and lifted up to give me a small hug.

"Jared. Your father is smart and we both hate him but you have his intelligence. Not the bad things in his mind but you have his mind. We can do this together. I can help build things. I can do whatever you need."

I didn't talk for a while and she grabbed my hand. "The girl you love is in there. She is trapped and she needs you. Don't give up on her. I am sick for her and why? Because I love her like a sister and you deserve a speck of happiness. You can't punish yourself forever for your mistakes." I cringed but she persisted on. "We have to stop this. We have to save what is left of the world and rebuild it; together?" she held out her hand. I looked at it for a moment and then glanced into her eyes.

"How sure are you that we can do this?" I asked.

She gulped and told the truth that I didn't want to hear. "Jared, we are the last people to save what is left of the world. We're the last people who give a damn." I took her hands in mine. "If not us, then who?"

"Holland, let's die trying." I said and I felt the raft being pulled over by a wave. It crashed down and I hovered my body over Holland's. We finally reached the land, and I helped her out of it.

She smiled to me. "While we're on this land, we have to recharge the pack. It recharges on it's own so no worries and then we will be out of here. That raft has a speed button so keep it safe." She hit the button, and it retracted back to its small shape.

She pulled out what appeared to be a million tiny gadgets from inside her pockets. Underneath her jeans, underneath her shirt, she took out a lot of things. "How did they never find those?" I said in shock. She laughed out loud.

"They become glued to my body and I hid them in places." I held up my hand to stop her.

"Enough info. Got you." She smiled and it seemed to pain her cheek because she instantly touched her cheek.

I cringed and she looked away quickly. I sat down on the ground and we began working frantically. I opened each gadget and began adjusting things on the insides. We had to make these weapons better and stronger than ever.

We weren't sure where we would end up, but we knew the war was just starting and that we would finish it. We had to. We would either die or save the entire world. If we did die, we hoped it would be for the greater good. The world would never be the same, but we had to salvage its remains.

*Taylor Hondos*

# Acknowledgements

Thank you to **my mom, my dad, Dina, Dimitri, Grandma, Susie, Great Grandmother and Yiayia** for giving me with the courage to write this book. I have many people to thank for the courage I have now.

I want to thank **Edee** for being there for me when I was still learning the ropes of book writing. I will always remember you and what you have done for me.

Thank you, **Ron** for taking my pictures. They are amazing and I can't thank you enough.

Thank you to my editor, **Measha,** for being awesome and my second pair of eyes. You let me know what worked and what didn't. You have changed the story in the best way possible.

Thank you to **Ashley** for listening to my vision. I could never have had my dream covers without you.

Thank you to my family for listening to me ramble on to you about wanting to write this book. All of you have believed in me and I'm blessed to have the biggest support system.

To my **mom**, who always told me to never give up even when I felt like I was going fail. You always told me I would make it happen if I put faith in myself first.

To my **dad**, who encouraged me and always believed in me, even when I was unsure.

To **Dimitri**, who always told me I could make it and that I was crazy not to try. And for always telling me that I will make it. I believe in you too. Your dreams will come true soon.

To **Dina**, who listened to me and encouraged me to do this. We both are going to do great things one day. I love you forever.

To **Grandma,** You always believed in me and you were so proud of me. I hope I still make you proud up there. I will see you again someday.

Finally, **thank you** for reading my books.

*Prospect*

# About the Author

**Taylor Hondos** attends the University of North Carolina at Greensboro, studying English Literature. In high school, she began writing "Antidote" and finished writing it by the end of her freshman year of college. "Prospect" is the second book in the Antidote trilogy. She plans to release "Corruption" next year. She lives with her family and adorable Miniature Schnauzer in North Carolina.

*Prospect*

www.ingramcontent.com/pod-product-compliance
Lightning Source LLC
Chambersburg PA
CBHW051458170626
46811CB00002B/533